O Monstrous World!

O Monstrous World!

Stories by

Josh Woods

Press 53
Winston-Salem

Press 53, LLC
PO Box 30314
Winston-Salem, NC 27130

First Edition

Cover design by Claire V. Foxx
and Kevin Morgan Watson

Cover art, "Textured Mask," Copyright © 2018
by Gatsi, licensed through iStock.

Library of Congress Control Number
2019933678

ISBN 978-1-95041-301-0

Iago: O monstrous world! Take note, take note, O world,
To be direct and honest is not safe.

—William Shakespeare, *Othello*

Grateful thanks to the editors of the following publications for first publishing these stories:

Apocalypse Now: Poems and Prose from the End of Days (Upper Rubber Boot Books, 2012): "The Lawgiver"

Black and Grey Magazine, August 2012: "New Days of the Wolf"

The Book of Villains (Main Street Rag, 2011): "Blackbeard in Repose" (as "Blackbeard Visits Seven Weeks")

Masque & Spectacle: An Arts and Literary Journal, December 2017: "A Theory of Game, A Theory of Horror"

Poor Yorick: A Journal of Rediscovered Objects (2018): "The Alchemist's Bench"

Press 53 Open Awards Anthology (2008): "The Exorcise Machine," First Prize in the 2008 Press 53 Open Awards for Genre Fiction

Prime Number Magazine, Issue 131, April-June 2018: "In Which Pinckney Benedict, Kermit Moore, and I Go A-Hunting for the Big Muddy Monster"

Surreal South '11 (Press 53, 2011): "He Who Fights with Monsters"

Surreal South '13 (Press 53, 2013): "Borges Lives in My Basement: Or, There Are More Things" (as "There Are More Things")

The Versus Anthology (Press 53, 2009): "Jesus VS. Thor"

XX Eccentric Women: Stories about the Eccentricities of Women (Main Street Rag, 2009): "Small Dead Monkey"

Contents

O Monstrous World!

A THEORY OF GAME,
A THEORY OF HORROR

I've played through this idea for a video game a dozen times at least, maybe close to a thousand, but because each run-through was distinct and only in my head, the number of times is both exact and unknowable, like Borges's *Argumentum Ornithologicum*: the proof of God through birds scattering in a dream. And in a video game, God is redundant.

My idea for this game is open-world, but restricted to a cozy little town in middle-America, a lot like Haddonfield, Illinois, a lot like my town, a place where husbands still go to the hardware store, one of those narrow old buildings along the downtown walkway. It's a town where wives still go to the local grocery owned by the fat-nosed old fellow who nips a little whiskey all day and flirts with just about every married momma who shops there but hasn't been subject to a good rumor of his success in many years. The place is a little repressive, sure, especially for those with different paradigms of thought, but it's honestly quite cute, with sidewalks and little sparrows everywhere, a town where high-school girls have outdated names and don't seem to know just how pretty they are, where they earn money by babysitting, even the smart ones, like the girl who babysits the little kids a few houses down. Her name is Connie. She doesn't know my name.

This video game will generate a town layout based on a few different map types populated with about a dozen models of structures with about a dozen variations each, for what we might call a "random" town each playing session, but it won't be truly random. Trying to convince a programmer to work with true randomness is a hopeless endeavor. Trust me. They're like, *Why would you want to do that? Junk in, junk out. No predictability. There's no design in that.* And I'm like, *No design? Are you kidding me? Randomness is the only path to true design. Look at the universe around you.* But he's like, *You're confusing contingency with causality and therefore missing the self-evident. If you observe well enough, there's always a pattern.* Then I'm like, *Don't tell me you're some kind of Bible-thumping Creationist all of a sudden. You think some celestial god is up there in the clouds shaping the spines on every unique snowflake? You think he's under every rock and leaf, watching your every move? You think he's the voice in your heart?* And then Donald's like, *Shut up and calm down* (because I had started yelling by then). *Listen, man,* he said. *Evolution works as an ordered system. Physics works as an ordered system, even when we don't have all the data. There are arbitrary features to it all, sure, but that's not the same as random chaos. What you're talking about is chaos. Actually, you always end up talking about chaos.* And that's enough to make me so mad that I decide to show him the difference, to show him some chaos with the closest sharp-edged item at hand across his smug face. But he wrestled it out of my hand before I could hit him with it—it was only a stapler, or I should say that it *was* a stapler when I had picked it up; I think it was a letter opener when he took it away from me—and then he kicked me out of his house for the last time. That was fine by me. I didn't want to work with him again either, because anyone who doesn't understand me doesn't deserve to work with me. I'm doing the opposite of chaos. I'm designing new realities. I'm peeling back the skin on this reality and looking at the working parts underneath, and taking them out, and with them, I'm creating worlds.

So at the start of the game, you choose your mask. Or one can be randomly selected for you. I don't want any setting for this part yet, like a walk-in closet or gallery or anything. No, when you acquire your mask, you should be in the Void. The options will include, of course, the famous whiteface mask of Michael Meyers—actually, I should call him The Shape—and the Jason goalie mask, and the Leslie Vernon frown mask, and the ghostface *Scream* mask—which was based on the painting by Edvard Munch, stolen twice under circumstances that have never been fully revealed. Copyright licenses will have to be sorted out for all those images, I'm sure. But there should be lots of other options: gas masks, clown masks, doll masks, plaster cast death masks, wolf masks, tiki masks, plastic burn masks, cannibal muzzle masks, ski masks, Venetian naso turco masks, boar masks, kabuki masks, Egyptian pharaoh masks, plague doctor masks, kaonashi no-face masks, leather stitched masks, Greek tragedy masks, Ku Klux Klan masks, fencing masks, Chinese demon masks, Saxon armored masks, jester masks, Batak funeral feast masks, Medieval public-humiliation masks, the Anonymous Guy Fawkes mask, the Red Death mask from the 1925 *Phantom of the Opera*, the stone smiley face mask from 7000 B.C., masks that look like the faces of real people, a mask that looks like me.

But don't get me wrong on that last one: a real human face is unacceptable. It must still be a mask. The mask is necessary. To have a face is to be human—or human*ized*—but the mask retrieves for us the other element, completing the pair of binary opposites: weighing the human against the inhuman. The scholar Elaine Pagels says as much in *The Origin of Satan*, "The social and cultural practice of defining certain people as 'others' in relation to one's own group may be, of course, as old as humanity itself. . .The distinction between 'us' and 'them' occurs within our earliest historical evidence, on ancient Sumerian and Akkadian tablets, just as it exists in the language and culture of peoples all over the world. Such distinctions are charged, sometimes with attraction, perhaps more often with repulsion—or both at once. The ancient Egyptian word for Egyptian simply means 'human'; the Greek word for non-Greeks, 'barbarian.'"

But the mask is also beyond mere human and inhuman. It is universal—of the universe. The original mask of The Shape in the 1978 *Halloween* was, because of their extraordinarily low budget, simply a retail mask of Captain Kirk that they painted white. While The Shape explored that little town of Haddonfield, going door to door like the angel in Egypt, visiting those high-school babysitters as the last face they would ever see, it was with the face of the discoverer, the man at the final frontier, the Dante of space, the one who would boldly go where no man has gone before.

At that point in the game, you will choose—or be randomly assigned—your outfit and weapon. The outfit options should be pretty basic, a kind of blank canvas in order to showcase the mask. Just a selection of coveralls and cloaks should be fine. Maybe we can throw some Freddy Krueger sweaters in there for fun, but, honestly, just a simple gray shirt and gray pants like I wear should suffice. And the weapon should be more like a style or tendency, some type to specialize in so that you can build skill sets with it, like the knife, the axe, the saw, the pick, something along those lines. But this skill path should not be restrictive. You should be able to pick up and use all sorts of randomized items in the game so that you can get innovative with weapons and ways to kill. It's a creative endeavor—to kill—and when any endeavor requires craft, persistence, *and* creativity, it's an art.

But just as you should be able to use the randomized items in your environment, so should your victims. Killing is not the only art in this game we're talking about. "Dying," says the Lady Lazarus, "is an art, like everything else." So let's say that, in this game, I stalk up behind a babysitter while she's cooking in the kitchen. I notice an iron trivet sitting on the countertop this time (I don't remember it being there last time) so I pick it up to use on her, but I accidentally scrape it across the countertop and alert her (no bonus points for me), and the young lady turns around to see me. Though she is terrified, she is able to fling the boiling hot pot of tomato soup at my face—at my mask, which was already red to begin with. It scalds, and while I'm blinded and distracted with pain, she gets away. I lose. So I have to begin again.

Reset.

But to be fair, not many babysitters will be that smart when the time comes. I bet Connie will.

Once game-play begins, there will be one other variable as well. No matter what any programmer says about the impossibility of randomness, this one will be an element that you can't see coming, even if it does follow a pattern. Here I'm talking about the able opponent. Cops exist in the town, but they're not what I would consider able opponents, for they have an all too mundane paradigm of thought. They'll respond sluggishly to 911 calls, assuming that all disturbances are either robberies for profit, teenage pranks for fun, or isolated errors under the influence of drugs, alcohol, or anger. They won't know how to understand you. And that's because they won't know why. The best they'll be able to do is guess that it was all for sick thrills, due to some mental illness, sexual perversion, or adrenaline addiction. But that will only be after the fact—in forensics—and that will be wrong.

No, the able opponent won't pose the same threat to you as the cops, who will merely exist to set parameters on how careless you can be through the night. The able opponent will be on the hunt specifically for you. He'll be the only one who gets how your mind works, and no one else will really believe him, an outcast in his own right. He would therefore be a mirror image of you if it weren't for some higher calling of his, some holy geis. And you won't get to select which kind of able opponent you'll get, or when he'll show up. At any point in the game—at the end, at the very beginning, maybe never—you'll be confronted with some kind of a Sam Loomis, an Abraham Van Helsing, a Saint George, a Beowulf, a Theseus, a Gilgamesh.

And as for your victims, you shouldn't get much credit for just killing people you happen to run across outside, like you do in those prosaic, unphilosophical crime/theft video games. You should have to enter their world somehow, which for most people in this town, at night, is their house. You should spend some time walking through the other yards to get to the right house. And at this point, when you are finally outdoors with your mask and your knife, looking for that right house, staying to the shadows, you find yet again that in this session the town is reordered, unrecognizable. It's not just the lingering, hot pain in your eyes, messing with your vision; no, it's truly reordered. You can't tell which house holds the babysitter you want, even though you've lived here for years and have walked these sidewalks at night more times than you can count. "I have been one acquainted with the night," as Frost puts it. But unlike Frost, I do not stop when I hear it, when I hear "an interrupted cry. . .over houses from another street," for that sound is created by me in the distance, taking her last breath, making it amplify greater than any breath she has ever taken—*created by me*, I should say, in another of these sessions. I don't know whether it's me in a session in the past or the future, or one I will ever play, only that it is certainly me, there, right now, in what the scholar Marie-Laure Ryan would call an Alternate Possible World. As she explains of Possible Worlds Theory, we can more successfully conceive of reality "as the sum of the imaginable rather than as the sum of what exists physically." At any given point we see through the immediate—the Actual World—while all that is imaginable is happening in Alternate Possible Worlds. Too often we anchor our typical human minds in that one Actual World, and my video game is showing me so much more.

But that scream I hear in the distance has now ended, and I still don't know where I am or where the house is that I want, so I must wander around, sliding between sheds and outbuildings, standing against fences until neighborhood dads are finished taking out the garbage, avoiding dogs because although I will kill them when they threaten to get loud and give me away, I get no credit for that. It's just not worth the effort, and I want it to be worth the effort. You always do. That's the whole point of this game.

And I get to the house that I'm pretty certain is the one she's babysitting in tonight—it has to be because it's so familiar to me—and I step softly on the hollow-sounding lava rocks in the landscaping under the windows, and I lift my head to look inside. The glass offers a weak ghost of a reflection of my mask, which is not the red one I just had on, but white, not one I've ever seen before, actually. And here she comes into view, strolling obliviously into the kitchen.

But it's not her, not the one I want. It's not even a babysitter. It's some wrong lady in the wrong house. Nevertheless, she can make for a good warm-up—a few extra points, maybe even a quick level-up—so I work my way as slowly as the weather itself to her back porch, and I open the screen door. The poorly fitted aluminum screeches at the hinges. The sound is not something I expected, and since it works against me, I should get docked some points.

I turn the knob on the door, which has been left unlocked for me, and I ready my knife, but now I see that it's not the knife I had chosen. It's just a clear plastic bag. I'm not sure what to make of this. It's heavy duty enough to withstand some struggling, and there are two handle-points for my grip, but I don't feel prepared to use it.

And that's when the porch light pops on.

I leap over the porch railing into the darkness, but I roll my ankle. I have a hard time moving without hissing in pain, so I huddle there.

The lady asks who is there, who it is, with her head high as if the night were going to answer.

And it will, for I leap with my good leg and net her head with the plastic bag. I pull her backward against the railing. She flails and gets a foot stuck between the pickets and is twisted back on herself, and I hang from the bag over her face. We balance like a scale. Her spine is the beam, and my body is the pan. I hang as if Osiris weighs my heart against the feather of Ma'at. If my heart is heavy in this, it will be devoured in the crocodilian mouth of Ammit, the god without worshippers. And my heart is not heavy in this.

When it is done, I walk away, onward through these reordered streets to seek the house I want, but I am slowed by this ankle. I need to inspect it, so I take the cover of some hedges, sliding down between their sharp combs. I should not have rolled my ankle. I let myself get thrown off by the randomized weapon. I won't let it happen again.

I know you're here, a voice says, much nearer than I could have expected.

I don't turn to look around for him. He's somewhere close enough nearby to see the rustle in the hedge if I make it, or to hear me again if I make any more noise. We are intimately close in this space, but we are only sounds to each other, like Yahweh calling to Abraham, calling to find him, and "behold," says Abraham, "here I am." And there he is indeed.

I'm putting an end to this, the voice says. *Tonight.*

It's my able opponent. He's found me. He's likely looking at the corpse on the porch right now, where she lies twisted with the plastic bag suctioned across her face. He's likely standing there with a revolver ready in his hand, scanning the area for me. And I worry that he's got me pinned down and beaten. I worry that I've lost this run-through. I worry that his voice sounds too familiar. I worry that it might be my own.

I know you're here, the voice says again.

He is right indeed—I am here—but he is so right that he is wrong: Behold, here I am. I am everywhere. And I shall begin again.

Reset.

And so I stand at the base of a tree in some schoolyard, in a newly strange town. The grid of streets has turned; the buildings have rotated and snapped into different spots; this Haddonfield shifts in my hand like a puzzlebox. And I must beware in my turning of its locks, lest I end up on the inside.

I take new paths down these sidewalks, into the neighborhoods, into the shadows. I have a phantom pain in my ankle, but that will not matter, for I'm feeling lucky this run-through. I'm going to find her.

As I stalk the streets, I glimpse another shape stalking as well, a gray form in a horrid mask. I hide out of sight until he passes and is gone. We must not encounter ourselves. I must not encounter myself.

So then I continue through the yards, in the shadows. Like the scattering birds I wind between the houses, drawn to the ones with light in the windows, trying to get a sense of the voices inside. There is no way that I can think of to indicate such feelings or instincts during gameplay, but I'm certain the right programmer can sort that out, and I'm certain my instinct is kicking in now. I pause at the house that feels right.

I spend some time walking the perimeter of her house—not hers, exactly, but the house she's babysitting in—spend some time stepping softly on the crisp, brown grass, staying against the vinyl siding except to work around the huge pile of leaves that haven't been bagged, avoiding the light of the powerline lamp there in the back yard by the out-building. I should consider trying the windows that are dark, windows to rooms that are for the moment abandoned, but first I should try the back door. And I do. I try the knob, but it's locked, as it should be. She's smart and safety-minded, Connie is.

So I pick a dark window at the back corner of the house, and at this point in the game, most of us would consider cutting the phone lines. It's something you see them do in the movies, and the game should accommodate such decisions

if you wish to see them through. You should get bonus
points for that kind of strategy—just a few—but these girls
all have cell phones now, so that won't be worth the effort.
You could cut the power to the entire house, and that would
be the right move for increasing her terror, but you don't
want this one terrified too soon. You don't want Connie
alerted. You want her to be calm and unaware as you stand
close to her, breathing, as close as a lover, just before the
moment comes.

You find a little garden spade nearby that hasn't been
used in months, not since it was warm, and you pry open
that window, for it was merely painted shut, not locked.
This takes a long while, a long while, requiring patience
and time not quite to the level of opening the door in "The
Tell-Tale Heart," but close to it. But you manage to ease it
up in silent segments, and then you pull yourself inside
and onto the floor of that abandoned bedroom at the back
of the house, into her world, without having made a single
human sound. That is essential for attaining the true
archetype of Horror. In the archetype of the Quest—the
binary opposite to Horror—the hero leaves home and
crosses the threshold into the Otherworld, where he
encounters strange beings while gaining allies, power,
accomplishments, and self-actualization. But the archetype
of Horror goes backward down that Maslow's Hierarchy
of Needs, losing self-efficacy and allies, all the way down
to the struggle for safety and survival. Rather than the
hero crossing the threshold into the world of the Other,
the Other crosses the threshold and invades the normal
world. This is not just pure theory. I turn the knob on the
bedroom door, and I creak open that door, and beyond
this threshold, I observe the normal world of this house,
the sound of the children watching a cartoon from some
living room down the hall, the sight of the low lamplight
toward the dining room, the smell of something cooking
on the stove for their supper. It smells like tomato soup and
grilled cheese, and Connie is talking on the phone to some
friend of hers about trying to buy a better used car than the

one she has, something reliable for going off to college. And the archetype of Horror is not mere theory, because I step across that threshold and stand there in the hallway, and no one in this world is yet aware that I have come. Behold, here I am.

From here, I can't tell what cartoon the children are watching, but I like to think that it's the 1955 Warner Brother's classic "One Froggy Evening," which most remember as featuring the "Hello, my baby, hello, my darling" frog. If they're not watching that one, they are now. In all sincerity, I believe it illustrates with stark purity the archetype of Horror. The cartoon begins with a blue-collar protagonist who demolishes a building, and in its ruins—in a sealed tomb that he pries open—he finds an ancient (undying) frog. The frog dances and sings. Thus the Other has crossed the threshold into the normal world. That the frog is a beast with a human voice is *Other* enough, Inhuman enough, but to amplify the Horror, no human voice other than the frog's is heard through the entire cartoon. When the human beings seem to speak to one another, they are muted behind glass; other times, they scheme and abuse each other wordlessly. Only the frog has voice. And the protagonist, with fantasies of ticket sales from sold-out shows of the frog's performances, is overcome by his own greed. Thus he breaks the second moral law of the Ancient Greeks as inscribed at Delphi, *mēdén ágan*, "nothing in excess," and welcomes his own decline down Maslow's Hierarchy, down to pure survival, and by his flaw has welcomed his own inevitable doom.

That flaw—along with its accompanying doom—is as necessary as the mask. It is implication. It makes up one half of the finality of Horror: *implication* and *inevitability*. The singing frog might be sealed away again, for now, but he will return; men of greed will pry him free once more, and always once more. He will always come again, for he is inevitable.

I don't know what Connie's flaw might be, but I know that her doom is inevitable.

I move down the hallway toward the kitchen. The living room is wide with a tall ceiling and a front door that is near the television the children are watching. I see the backs of their little heads, and they don't see me. I'm not even a shadow in the corner of their eyes. I don't exist to them yet, but I'm there, right behind them. When this session is over—and I shall indeed let them pass through this session alive—in this Alternate Possible World their parents will finally have to explain death to them. *It's always there, right behind you,* they'll tell the children. *It always was. You just didn't know it. And what he has done for you— what he has done for all of us in this quaint little town—is to lift the veil. The Ancient Greek word for this lifting of the veil was* ἀποκάλυψις *, "apocalypse,"* they will say to the children. *He has delivered unto us apocalypse.*

At the edge of the kitchen door, I hear Connie bright and clear now. She walks back and forth over the meal she is preparing, still talking on the phone not about boys or sex or gossip or shopping, but about grants and scholarships, majors, transfer credits, the sensible elements of the all-too-assumed future. I didn't expect that of her, but I should have known. And there is no way to know whether she will happen to be facing my direction if I turn the corner and enter the kitchen with her. I could just peek quickly, but that would alert her just the same if she were facing my way, and it would be sheepish of me, an action suited for the timid, for the lambs that ought to be painted across such doorways. So I boldly go.

I stand in the kitchen with her. Her back is to me. She works with bread on the countertop, with her phone pinched to her ear by a shrugged shoulder. The refrigerator beside me kicks on audibly, but this does not garner any reaction out of her. She has worked as a babysitter in this house for many months now. She is used to the sounds it makes, to the sounds it does not make.

Now is the time for me to ready my weapon, but this time I forgot to select one, or to have one randomly selected for me. I am empty-handed.

Next to the refrigerator, on the counter far from her but within reach of me, there is no trivet this time, but there is a block of kitchen knives. So I take a larger handle at the top of the block, and I slide it out, imagining that the sound it makes has a slick sheen to the ear and that—though my drawing of the knife actually makes no sound—it ought to be there in the video game. So it makes the sound indeed.

And then I step closer to her.

She laughs about something said to her over the phone. I can hear the muffled voice of the person on the other end—that's how close I am to Connie.

This gore will not be unnatural, merely inevitable. As we are reminded in the "Apocalyptic Narrative" of poet Rodney Jones: "Listen, only a thin layer of skin / Keeps us from squirting into the world." The only question is which world that will be.

But I don't raise the knife just yet. I want to stand this close for a moment longer. Her hair is right under my nose. I close my eyes and try to smell her slowly. And I do. The video game won't be able to include smells, and I realize now what a tragedy that is. So I pause the game.

I take in through my nostrils what no one else will ever be able to.

My nostrils are outside of time. And they have life in them.

And when that's over, when I open my eyes again, she is looking right up at me. Her face is frozen, her eyes bright, her mouth only just beginning to tremble, the subtle beginnings of an avalanche, her mind beginning to slip from the Actual World she was in, to the Alternate Possible World she is in now.

Now is when I lift the knife. I lift it above her, with clear demonstration, making sure to catch our reflection in it, the both of us together, the fleeting image of the girl and the mask. The girl's face is so familiar in that quick mirror, but my mask shuffles through a thousand faces faster and faster at random. My mask is the Iroquois False-Face mask, the six-eyed Oni mask, the black mourning veil, the red Speaker of the Sea mask, a motorcycle helmet, the Frankenstein's

Creation mask, faster and faster, the Dia de los Muertos
sugar-skull mask, a drape of chains, the mask of Itzpapalotl,
the joint-surgeon face-shield mask, the carnival grotesque
mask, the Man in the Iron Mask, faster and faster, a mask
of purple and thorn, the two-faced mask of Janus, the great
bascinet helmet, the mask of Nyarlathotep, an eldritch mask
I cannot name, a mask that has no face but is not blank, a
mask of all colors, a mask of none. I can't keep up with
them—they shuffle so fast—and I can't help but watch the
glitching permutations, mesmerized, my face scattering
before me like an uncountable flock.

But she hits me with something heavy in the solar plexus,
even before she screams. And she slides away to the side.
I'm hurt—my in-game health meter drops—but I'll be fine.
I catch the back of her sweater—a pale wedding-like
color—before she manages to flee the kitchen. I have a
good grip on it, so I take just a second to breathe once or
twice. She had knocked some of the air out of me. I see
what she hit me with: a cast-iron trivet lies on the floor.
Connie had reached out and found what didn't exist in
this session, and she used it against me. She's innovative.

She's screaming at the children, telling them to leave
through the front door, to run to the neighbor's house. She
doesn't tell them to call the cops—which would have added
further confusion to their little minds—just to run and save
themselves.

With her caught in my hand, I bring the knife up for a
slice into her tenderloin along her spine, but she turns and
makes a grab for the knife. Though she gets hold of it too,
that will make no difference: I have leverage here and can
bring the blade down on her regardless. But she guides it
down with me, and we end up cutting through the fabric
of her sweater together like a cake.

Now I just have a ball of sweater in my hand, and she's
free, and she takes off down the hallway, away from the
front door, away from the direction the children are fleeing.
She must be trying to bait me away from them, the babysitter
with the heart of gold.

I follow her not with a rush—because of the phantom ankle—but with a steady march. She turns a corner, making clattering noises, making a sound of terror that isn't so much a scream anymore as an ignoble bleat, which is unfortunate for this moment, aesthetically. I give her just a second to stop that noise, which I do not want to hear, and then I continue. I make my way around the corner too, and I don't see her or hear her now, but to my left is a staircase leading up to the second floor, and to my right is the back door now standing wide open.

Which way?

This is where true Game Theory comes into play. What we have in this moment is a zero-sum game with two players, both of us with what is called *imperfect information.* We can call this scenario "The Game of Connie's Ubiety." She must be somewhere—her position being both exact and unknown—and she can be in only one of two directions: Did Connie open the back door and flee outside as it appears? Or did she open the back door as a diversion and instead flee upstairs? Should I go outside, or upstairs? A zero-sum game with two players and two options creates a strategic form game matrix of four Alternate Possible Worlds:

1. I go outside, and Connie went outside. For Connie, her choice would have been left obvious to me, relinquishing her advantage afforded by my imperfect information. In this Alternate Possible World, I have time to spot her, catch her, and kill her. I win.

2. I go outside, but Connie went upstairs. For Connie, this would be the ideal scenario, the purpose of her (possible) diversion. In this Alternate Possible World, I waste time trying to find where she went outside, much more time than I would have spent searching the enclosed upper floor of the house. In that uncertain time—ten minutes, maybe more—Connie could take numerous defensive actions or alternate escape routes before I finally make my way back to the house and up the stairs, and I probably lose.

3. I go upstairs, and Connie went upstairs. For Connie, this was her necessary gamble in hopes of the better scenario in which I am fooled (2, above). In this Alternate Possible World, I catch her and kill her. I win.

4. I go upstairs, but Connie went outside. For Connie, this would be an unexpected move on my part, thus not one that she had prepared to take advantage of. In this Alternate Possible World, I search the upstairs quickly enough, and then go back downstairs and outside, likely with enough time to track her, catch her, and kill her. I win.

Just like the Battle of the Bismarck in 1943 between American and Japanese forces, there is no dominant strategy equilibrium, but through the process of eliminating dominated strategies for both of us—assuming both players are rational in that they choose intelligent options, and Connie is such a player—there does end up being a weak-dominance equilibrium: North–North in 1943, Upstairs–Upstairs right now.

I run upstairs.

There she is.

She stands ready to fight me, for, behold, here I am.

Behind her in the master bedroom, the closet is open, and all the dresser drawers are open, and clothes are flung everywhere. She had been looking for a gun—hoping for one—but all she holds is a baseball bat. It appears that the owners of this house subscribed to the inexplicable urban myth of the home-defense baseball bat. There are likely numerous explanations for why such people invest their faith so foolishly—they are probably the same kind who pray to that celestial god in the clouds—but the only hypothesis that comes to my mind at the moment is that, as historian Jacques Barzun says, baseball is Quest, an odyssey away from Home, around the known world in danger, and back again, so the bat must seem like the hero's archetypical sword.

To avoid Bulverism, according to C.S. Lewis, I need to demonstrate not *why* I am right but *that* I am right in the uselessness of a bat. She readies for a swing with not enough room to complete it, of course, and I kick her wrists. The bat drops from her hands.

I grab her throat and charge forward with her, pinning her to the bed. She can't get away now. She's on her back. Her throat is clutched. Her legs are pinned under mine. Her scratching fingers are useless.

With my other hand I want to raise the knife, but it is so much heavier now. I look, and it's not the knife I just had. It's a little pronged spear, a golden trident maybe, or a kind of large, barbed arrow catching the glint of lights that I cannot find. I don't know what to call this thing other than *random*. But it's not truly random—as it would be if it were suddenly a bathtub, or a pomegranate, or a river of oil—no, it's still a weapon, so although it's arbitrary, it follows a pattern. Donald was right, even here.

But that is no matter. I am over Connie with this trident, and she swoons before me, for what I bring her is not death but ecstasy. This is how it always is, and this is why we are meant to fit together, killer and victim, celestial and terrestrial, in perfect harmony. This is the transverberation of the Ecstasy of Saint Teresa of Avila, and we, like she, are in a marble moment of eternity. I can hear her speak it now not with her voice but in her own head, before it happens, quoting Saint Teresa of Avila, *I saw in his hand a long spear of gold, and at the iron's point there seemed to be a little fire. He appeared to me to be thrusting it at times into my heart, and to pierce my very entrails; when he drew it out, he seemed to draw them out also, and to leave me all on fire with a great love of God.*

And I welcome her thanks, and I consider where to pierce her first, and from what angle, and where to draw it out and begin again. There are so many ways to complete this, so many slices, so many patterns, some geometric, some random, so many patterns that were there to be cut into her body from the beginning of time, even if there had been no way of predicting it, though it was inevitable. I opt for something clean and direct, to plunge the trident straight down into her heart. So I prepare the lift, and that's when I hear the voice in my head, something I was not expecting, *Don't do it. Let her go. Get away from her.*

It is a voice as familiar as a mirror, but it cannot be. I do not hear my own heart beating under the floorboards, where I would have hidden it—after cutting it out of my chest—so that it would tell no tale. No, it is the voice of another. Or is that not right? Did I indeed? Is it my own voice indeed?

Keeping Connie pinned, I turn to see.

It's Donald.

He stands at the bedroom door, and he has that revolver. It's aimed and ready for me.

I knew I'd find you here, he says to me. *I always did. And I always will. We are a pattern, you and I.*

I lunge off the bed to stab him, but he shoots. And he shoots again. I fall back. I can't tell whether I'm hit. I don't quite feel the wounds, but maybe they're there. I'm backed up against the window pane, and that's when Connie gets up and shoves me with all her might.

I break through.

I fall.

I hit a pile of dry leaves, the leaves I have seen before. I roll out and take off running into the night. But I need not worry. I can rest and recover. This Haddonfield is a fine and private place, and I have world enough and time. This is not Game Over. I'll come back, and I always will, and I was always going to. I'll shift this puzzlebox in my hand once again, this place that surrounds me like scattering birds in a dream. I have done this in the past and in the future a number of times that is exact and unknowable, so in theory, this is infinite. Behold, here I am. I am everywhere. I am inevitable.

Reset.

HE WHO FIGHTS WITH MONSTERS

". . .should be careful, lest he thereby become a monster."
—Nietzsche, *Beyond Good and Evil*

He sits studying his hands front and back, those limbs wrapped and taped as solidly as casts from fingers to forearms, the wrapwork bulging grotesquely from the brass knuckles underneath, an advantage that doesn't really bother anyone in the crowd, or anyone in the promotion, or even anyone in the other corner for that matter, being that he fights living, breathing monsters in this underground circuit, and that his own human figure squared off against such beasts makes a thing like using brass knuckles seem excusable, even expected, yet his hands seem distant somehow, not doing any good in his effort to remember just how it was he got himself to this point in life.

These days, the fighting is just for the cash. These monster fights have been big money so far, and tonight's fight against a thing they brought in from Germany will be the biggest purse so far. They billed it as, "Man VS Monster, Real UFC Vet Ivan Troupes Fights Terror of the Black Forest—The Doppelganger!" His handlers, who have been saving up his money for him, tell him that this fight tonight will be against a very familiar body-type— in other words, it'll be a fight against a creature with a mostly human anatomy. And a win tonight should be enough cash to get him far away from all this, away from this concrete fight-pit, away from this burnt-out bourbon distillery and its foul crowd of cash-waiving hillbillies and gun-toting bookies, far away from eastern Kentucky. It'll get him off of this canvas cot, where he has recurring nightmares of what seem to be formless terrors from the deep past, and it'll get him out of this dark, dank cell of a room. It'll be a chance to become a completely different person, which he wants so badly that he sits, a pugilist at rest, searching the weird sight of his hands for some reminder of who he really is and must have been.

He remembers, surely, his fighting in the UFC in the early days, before they had the phrase "mixed martial arts," before they had the cable channel deals and the reality shows and the preponderance of rules such as being forced to wear gloves or being penalized for striking the groin. Well, he remembers at least watching the videos of himself fighting. His tale-of-the-tape read, "Ivan Troupes, 6 feet 3 inches, 218 pounds, 77.5-inch reach." Thick-shouldered yet slim-chested, a bearded face but a hairless body, he could have hailed from the Bronze Age. He studied the fight videos of himself skipping sideways around the cage and then switching his trajectory as swift as some airborne thing, shooting in for the clinch, locking up the other fighter despite wild struggles, like Menelaus to Proteus, and then lifting for a skull-first slam into the mat. He was good. His current handler says that if the UFC hadn't cut him over his refusal to take a dive for the sake of the bracket setup and for pay-per-view overrun time, if he hadn't been forced to fight in the even shadier promotions in Japan where he finally got blacklisted, the once-great Ivan Troupes could have been a legitimate belt-holder. His name could have been in the Hall of Fame with Royce Gracie and Ken Shamrock and Dan Severn and the rest of the old-schoolers. Instead, he has ended up in an illegal racket fighting all manner of unnatural beasts, which he needs no videos to recall clearly. His first fight here, as he remembers well, had been against a troll from Wales.

◆ ◆ ◆

The Welshmen had kept the troll covered with an army-green tarp, which must have functioned like some sort of hawk hood because the troll seemed to be doing nothing under there except breathing calmly, despite all the noise. The crowd roared and spit and cursed; the announcer bellowed from his bullhorn, something about this troll hailing from under the second oldest bridge in Britain, something about its steady diet of children. Ivan just bounced on his toes, side to side, thinking only of a quick, sharp knockout so he wouldn't have to grapple with that monster. It wasn't until the other men cleared out of the concrete pit and yelled "fight," not until they yanked a rope to withdraw the tarp, did Ivan worry about what the troll looked like.

It crouched on its haunches like some primitive old-worlder telling stories by a fire, and its features were impossibly swollen. It could have been some exaggerated primate, fur-covered, with a mane at its neck and liver spots on its bald patches, were it not for its head-to-feet, odobenine slickness. The troll's fingers dripped with its own spit and snot. Its eyes glowed blue, but they weren't enlarged or piercing like he would have expected of a monster, not wicked or searching. They were close and small, too much so.

Ivan decided to wait on his side of the concrete pit and to keep hopping, to stay loose, so that the troll would have to move first and reveal how it went about attacking things. Soon it slouched forward, helping itself walk every few steps with its hands. It seemed to approach Ivan as if he were a passive meal set out for easy consumption, a steak for a gator, and when it reached out slowly to take Ivan by the skull, he slid out, circled the troll before it could lumber around, and launched a flying knee into its spine. The troll fell forward and lay there hacking and wheezing.

The crowd cheered. Ivan raised his arms. Even if he hadn't ended the fight just yet, he knew at least that a win was inevitable. He was simply too fast for it, and he wondered for an instant if monsters like this one had aided in the evolution of the human body millennia ago, requiring it to become the fastest of the apes.

The troll, still coughing and hacking, turned toward Ivan. It had its arm down its own throat, elbow deep. Bile leaked down its fur and spilled on the floor. It kept hacking and reaching deep into its own guts; then it withdrew its arm and, in its hand, held out the severed head of a young girl. Her face had been wrenched in a perpetual cry, silent yet full of pain, her skin having been turned a weird gray from digestive juices, her long, curled hair soaked but otherwise golden blond. The troll threw the head at Ivan, who was so shocked by the sight of it that he stood unmoving and was hit in his mouth.

He fell. The little dead girl's skull had hit him like a bowling ball, busting his jaw and cracking his teeth. The taste of its fluids twisted his guts. The stench was yellow. He rolled on the ground wiping his mouth, and spat, and shook his head to regain his wits.

Then the troll was upon him.

It lay heavily on him and tried to corral Ivan's arms and legs, perhaps in an effort to roll him up into a shape that would fit easily down its throat. It made the huffing sounds of a pervert, a rapist, and it grabbed at him just as eagerly. Ivan writhed and kicked. On his back, he managed the semblance of an open guard, jiu-jitsu style, and he arm-dragged the troll off-center just enough to create an escape for himself. He slid away and scrambled up to all fours, his hand clutching a mess of golden curls. Then he stood with it and felt the weight of the little girl's head hanging at the end of its hair like a medieval ball on a chain. He grinned.

The troll roared and turned slowly to him, ready to pounce now, ready now to attack full-on.

Ivan rolled his grip and twisted the hair one turn tighter; then he began swinging it, bringing it faster and faster into a deadly swirl. He stepped carefully, checked his distance with the other hand outstretched, then whipped the little girl's head down onto the troll's face.

Something split. Blood sprayed centrifugally. Ivan twirled the girl's head back to full velocity and struck again.

The troll curled up now, and Ivan stood one foot on the beast, beating it over and over. When it was no longer clear which flying chips of bone belonged to the dead girl and which to the troll, when the head at the end of its hair no longer looked human, when the troll had ceased twitching with each hit, Ivan stopped. The crowd wailed with delight. Both sets of cornermen and handlers and equipment shufflers and managers rushed in and lifted Ivan aloft, men's hands reaching up to him in apotheosis. Someone cried, "I can't wait to see what they make him fight next!"

And he did continue to fight. He fought a chupacabra, a giant Chinese caterpillar, a were-cow from India that they billed as a minotaur, and, the worst of them all, a goblin. That goblin, the furry little sucker, was supposed to be a cushion fight, something to get folks feeling safe enough with putting money on the winner that they would gamble on the length of the fight, or on the manner in which Ivan would finish it. Instead, as soon as they opened the goblin's cage, it climbed out of the pit and took off into the crowd, attacking the onlookers, lacerating their skin, slicing achilles tendons, leaping from one set of shoulders to the next and biting plugs out of their scalps, latching onto their crotches and chomping away. The crowd had torn loose. It was pandemonium. The bookies fumbled with their decommissioned assault rifles and took pot-shots at the goblin, but they wounded only the people who ran and swarmed in every direction, arms flailing, unable to find a working exit.

Ivan climbed into the crowd and shoved his way toward the ever-moving sprays of blood until he caught up with the nasty little thing. It was busy cleaning its way through some guy's shoulder, its teeth digging as fast as a bandsaw, the guy screaming and dancing in a helpless circle. Ivan loaded up for a heavy right hand, waited for the victim to swing around one more time, and he knocked the goblin senseless. Then he pulled it down to the ground by its leg, stepped on its neck, and gave that leg a sharp tug. He felt it snap. He lifted the lifeless goblin up like wild game and yelled to the crowd that he got it.

All those who were free of serious injury cheered wildly for him. Even some of the wounded uttered cursing thanks. They had paid him to be an entertainment, and he had done that. They had wanted him to be ruthless and fearless, and he had been. When, in need of a hero, they wanted him to save them from their own monster, he had. He could be anything they wanted him to be.

So Ivan stops searching the strange sight of his own wrapped hands because the men tell him it's fight-time. He stands, shakes out the tension in his limbs, pops his neck, and follows his handlers through the corridor. They lead him between the crowd held back by sawhorses, and down into the fight pit through a hatch opening in the newly constructed cage dome—a creaking, metalwork, web-like structure which the promoters understood now, after the goblin incident, to be necessary. As awkward and as makeshift as that cage dome looked, it seemed strong enough to keep out all but the most unimaginable terrors, those of his nightmares, which would never be put in the fight-pit in the first place.

Ivan doesn't want to bother looking toward his opponent, the monster, because he's seasoned, because he now knows that first impressions don't end up affecting the fight, because if it's going to be a surprise no matter what—as it always is—then anticipating nothing will make him invulnerable to surprise. He doesn't even want to bother listening to the announcer or to his own cornermen or to the opposing cornermen. But their noise gets in his ears anyway.

"In this corner, what you've all been waiting for." The announcer screams through his bullhorn. "Real-life UFC veteran Ivan Troupes!"

Ivan bounces on his toes side-to-side as he always does, looking down at the filthy concrete beneath him, trying hard to think nothing, to hear nothing, to see nothing.

The crowd's cacophony is all static.

"And his opponent, the terror of the Black Forest, the mirror of fears, the monster you all know too well: The Doppelganger!"

Ivan can't help it. He looks up to the far side of the fight pit to see the monster. And he sees himself. It is him. It's exactly himself in every way: the build, the face, the side-to-side bounce. Its face looks just as shaken by the uncanny sight as his own must, the only difference, a slight one, being that it looks older, not the younger face so familiar from his old fight videos.

And that's when the realization hits him, and it sends his head reeling, a flash of a thousand lost thoughts, a sudden upside-down feeling, like the snag of a net in a dark forest.

The men clear the pit and call a start to the fight, but he stands inert in shock. The other Ivan Troupes rushes to him and batters him with immediate hooks and overhands and looping kicks. He covers up and crumples. He receives the blows despite his attempt to shield himself from them, and they hurt, but a deeper anguish overwhelms him. He feels betrayed and, in that instant, indignant. He can hear the humans screaming for Ivan to kill The Doppelganger, and he knows now that they mean him, and he knows now that it is true.

And he can feel his suffering—this revelation—taking hold of his body, changing him. He feels the real Ivan Troupes halt his attack for a moment. He feels himself growing larger, his back pressing against the cage-dome ceiling, straining the chain links and popping the welded pipe joints loose. He stretches his proportions out from the confines of the man he was mocking, his limbs unwinding and multiplying, his face unhinging. Men in the crowd are scattering with nowhere to go. He looks down with spreading eyes to see the real Ivan Troupes reset himself for battle, chin down, hands up, as bold as he was ever mimicked to be, but he will not let these men see another victory for an Ivan Troupes against some hapless beast. No, he will reflect something else for them now, transforming into something far worse than any here have ever seen, into something from the recesses of history, from the old abyss, giving shape to an ancient terror these men have forgotten.

THE LAWGIVER

Grüt lifted his voice from among the throng and swore his axe to protect the lawgiver, who had no beard. Thus it was settled. The lawgiver was allowed to step off the bow of the boat onto their shore and speak any words without fear because it was clear that the might of Grüt would quickly fall on any man who would be the lawgiver's killer.

The lawgiver looked out from the shadows of a heavy hood and spoke with a fair voice, saying only, "I am a man who deceives you not when I say that I am very tired and hungry from this journey."

Rak, the brother-in-law of Huhlik Ford and the father of Stom, said, "We did not pay such a heavy wage for a lawgiver just to listen to bellyaching."

Hagnov Ford, the son of Huhlik Ford, said, "Yes, let him speak a doom on the killers of our cousin Hagik before I take my rightful vengeance and wet these rocks under our boots with the blood of the Sturlsons."

Stag Lock, the man who had brought the boat ashore and who was the elder uncle of the three Sturlson brothers, said, "What is this news about Hagik?"

Wrot, the father-in-law of Hagik, said, "While you were past the horizon, my daughter was made a widow, and her two sons were made orphans, and the only sheath that has stayed the blades of the Fords has been the sight of your boat returning with a lawgiver, so let it be the lawgiver who tells now us how the Sturlsons must die."

The lawgiver said, "I have not come here to speak of killing for killing. And even so, we first must discover for certain who killed this Hagik."

Gunner Sturlson, who spoke also for his two younger brothers, said, "We killed him."

Gam Sturlson, the younger brother of Gunner, said, "Yes. Hagik had killed our uncle Geir. Both men died good deaths. Hagik carried three of our swords deep in his ribs, and still he fought. We clubbed him with logs until our arms tired."

Many of the men nodded to one another because this news was good to their ears.

Gunner Sturlson said, "Thus we stand ready for any hand ready for us. We even stand ready for the words of this lawgiver, who looks built out of kindling, frail enough to be broken by a bird's beak."

Many of the men laughed.

Hagnov Ford said, "Then let this lawgiver loose his tongue, or my knife will loose it for him." Hagnov grabbed the chest of the lawgiver's cowl, and surprise struck Hagnov's face.

A sudden light swung across the crowd, and the gleaming axe of Grüt came down through the wrist of Hagnov, severing his hand as smoothly as though it were made of goat cheese. The lawgiver fell to the rocks and, while holding back a scream with a trembling hand, crawled backward from the severed fist that clung still to the cowl's blood-soaked wool.

Grüt said, "My axe was clearly offered to the lawgiver. Thus my axe was offered to the hand that threatened him. Are there any who argue against me?"

No man argued against him.

Grüt said, "Thus there will be no vengeance against me for chopping off Hagnov's hand."

Urli, the cousin-in-law of the Sturlsons, who held a bow at his hip and kept an arrow nocked on the bowstring, said, "All are agreed to this, but the lawgiver must still speak."

Grüt said, "How can you demand a hardy mouth of words to echo from a hollow gut? Who among you is as frail and unfed as he? The lawgiver will come to my home, and I will feed him so that he will regain his strength, and at tomorrow's dawn we will meet at the Ironbones to hear his words."

The other men said, "Then we will go to our homes in the Sheltered Valley until we meet tomorrow."

And all men did what they said they would do.

Just before dawn, Grüt led the lawgiver, whom he had hoisted onto his ox, through the snows and hills toward the Ironbones. While they traveled, the law-giver spoke little, but Grüt spoke of many stories of the places they passed.

Grüt said, "That is the house of the widow Helva who slaughtered one of her hogs and found a troll in its belly. The troll fled into the nearby wood, yonder." And Grüt said, "On the far ridge there is a ghost who walks at night and who cries lamentations. We laugh at him." And Grüt said, "Those stone trunks once held aloft a road for the old gods. They once traveled roads made of a single slab of stone that would stretch on and on for days. When I was young, I asked my father where the old gods found a single slab of stone as long as this, and he broke my jaw for my insolence."

The lawgiver said, "They were not gods; they were only people. And they lived under rule of law, and law gave them the ability to make wonders, wonders even greater than those roads."

Grüt said, "They were certainly gods."

The lawgiver said, "No. They were only people."

Grüt laughed. He said, "I believe that you are wise, my small beardless one, but you do not know our land."

The lawgiver said, "That I do not," but the lawgiver had more than one meaning to those words.

◆ ◆ ◆

Grüt led the ox and the lawgiver into the thick winter mist of the White Valley. He said to the lawgiver, "We travel now across the frozen lake that is called Tyr. Have no fear for your life about this. Your fingers could not touch the water below even if you reached into an ice hole to the depth of your shoulder."

The lawgiver said, "Why do we travel on a frozen lake?"

Grüt said, "So we may reach the Ironbones before the others and take the high ground."

The lawgiver said, "I do not want any more fighting."

Grüt said, "There has been no fighting since you stepped ashore." Then Grüt halted the ox and with great swiftness withdrew his axe with which he had cut off Hagnov's hand. He said, "I have spoken too quickly. Listen."

From the white mists ahead of them came the sounds of metal kissing metal in battle. And then came the screams of men.

Grüt said to the lawgiver, "Stay on the ox." Then he lifted his axe above his head and roared and ran forward into the mist.

The lawgiver called after Grüt to stop, but the mists swirled closed behind Grüt. The lawgiver spurred the ox forward, and the ox trotted its hooves quickly across the ice. The lawgiver halted the ox near enough to see Grüt entering the battle that already filled the White Valley with its noise.

There on the frozen lake called Tyr, the three Sturlson brothers made their final stand against five Fords and four other men who grieved for Hagik. Hagnov Ford stood back from the fight, still holding wrappings over his severed wrist, and yelled, "Give them your blades. Send them to the Frozen Hall where Hagik awaits his killers."

Grüt sprinted forward and slid across the ice and leveled the blade of his axe and, as he sped by, lopped off the head of Hagnov Ford, who was between words, and slid farther still and lopped off the head of Wrot.

Rempt, the brother of Hagnov Ford, screamed at this

and thrust his spear through the meat of Grüt's thigh and dug the point of the spear into the ice, and thus Grüt stopped sliding.

Grüt swung his axe at Rempt but could not reach him. Behind Rempt, Gunner Sturlson lifted his wooden mace and flattened Rempt's skull.

Grüt struggled to wedge the spear out of his thigh as he watched Gunner Sturlson's stomach slit open by a sword and spill onto the ice. Gunner's younger brother Gam leapt into the path of an arrow meant for his younger brother Paith, and the arrow pierced him through the neck and stuck there, but Paith was struck at the shoulder by an axe that dug deeply into his chest. Gam became berserked. He swung his sword wildly, but because of the arrow in his throat he could not roar, so his enemies did not fear his rage, and they hacked his arms away and broke his knees and let him bleed dry on the ice.

Grüt managed to free the spear from his leg, and he threw the spear, and it brought down one of the men, Yorn, who was the nephew of Hagnov Ford, but the other men backed far enough away from Grüt so as not to be struck by anything he could throw. Rak said, "Grüt, the fight is ended this morning, and no man here wants to fight with you. We will meet you at the Ironbones to hear the lawgiver's words."

Grüt said, "Who will send word to the women to gather and burn the fallen men?"

Stom, who was the son of Rak, said, "I will go tell the women. And first I will tell Sana, the sister of the three Sturlson brothers."

Rak said, "Yes. And tonight we will cook our food over the fires of these men's corpses as we sing great songs of their lives while the women wail for them."

And Stom departed back toward the Sheltered Valley, and the other men departed toward the Ironbones. And Grüt bandaged his wound and leaned on the neck of the ox like a yoke and led the lawgiver, who remained silent, onward toward the Ironbones.

* * *

On the hill where the Ironbones protruded from the earth, the men had gathered and waited and spoke of the many wars that had been announced at the Ironbones. They also spoke of wonder at what laws they would receive in this same place. The Ironbones leaned so heavily that at every hour it cast a shadow in the snows, and it was in this shadow that the men stood, so when the day came when the Ironbones would finally crash down, it might crush them under its glory in remembrance of the old gods who must have been likewise crushed under the glory of their own cities.

Grüt parted the crowd and led the ox and the lawgiver to the hill that overlooked the men. The lawgiver balanced on the thick back of Grüt's ox, feet steadying on its spine, and stood on it with grace, and spoke across the crowd of men with a voice that rang like music against the beams and angles of Ironbones. The lawgiver said, "Silence, all of you. This morning I have been witness to the cruelty and blindness of this land. I will speak quickly and plainly, for you must understand this now. I give you one law only, and as you hear it, so it shall be burned into your brains: None shall take vengeance."

The crowd remained silent. A brief wind dusted snow across the men and whitened their hair and their beards. The men gave no sign that they would accept these words.

The lawgiver said, "None shall take vengeance. And I shall tell you why: blood lost is never regained by blood spilled. Each vengeance you take only demands more vengeance in its place. I know you see the instability of your land. That is why your elders paid your unearthed treasures to the Far Temple for me, a lawgiver, but you have not seen the simple reason for your problems. Think of this: if the first finger of the hand breaks the second finger, and for this offence the third finger breaks the first finger, then how can the hand wield a sword in its own defense?"

Stag Lock said, "My grandfather wielded a sword with a hand so broken that from his skin protruded three bones, and their hollow tips whistled in the wind as he swung his sword, and he killed six men before he fell to the sword of his wife, my grandmother, who was an angry woman and who was against him on that day."

The lawgiver said, "But do you understand this law?"

Rak said, "We understand this law, but then what harm shall we inflict on those who kill the beloved members of our families?"

The lawgiver said, "No harm at all. No harm. Instead the killer will announce himself, as I see it is your way to do, and he will pay tributes to the family for his entire life to replace the foods and goods and labor that were lost by the killing. This is the only way to repair your families and cease your circle of death."

The men were silent, and across their faces many brows furrowed with trouble. Clanks of metal among the men spoke their disquiet when the men would offer no words from their mouths. No one yet spoke of killing the lawgiver over dislike of this law, but they looked as though they might.

The lawgiver looked down from the ox and whispered, "Grüt?"

And, for the first time, Grüt felt overwhelmed by the eyes of the lawgiver, and by the gentle features of the lawgiver's face, and Grüt felt very strange about this. Then Grüt said to the crowd, "I see unrest among you, but it is in vain because I ask you this: does any man have wiser words this morning than those of the lawgiver? If so, let him speak now and boldly."

No man spoke.

The lawgiver said, "This is good. You and your families are now on the path that will lead you to the glorious ways of the ones you call the old gods."

Many men nodded at this talk of the old gods, and thus they departed toward their homes, and the sun set that day without another death.

After the moon had changed once and many payments and many labors had been accumulated over killings, making many men feel the hardships of paying these tributes while providing for themselves, there came a piece of good news, which rang out from valley to valley: there would be a wedding between Stom and the sister of the three Sturlson brothers, whose name was Sana.

All agreed that the wedding should be on the night of the solstice and that it should be the grandest wedding of the year because the harsh winter nights would begin to wane, and the valley snows would lessen, and the elk would herd nearer, and the union of these two families would mean an end to many tributes.

There were other joys as well. Both Stom and Sana were brought to blushing at the mention of the other. And the men slapped Stom on his back and on his face and offered him livestock in trade for his wedding night, and Stom kicked snow at them and laughed. And every day the virgins combed the hair of Sana and crushed sweet pine needles over her shoulders and then went home to comb their own hair in the way of Sana's hair.

And on the day before the wedding, Rak and Grüt dragged stone seats into the Great Hall of the Sheltered Valley in preparation. They were alone, for even the lawgiver, who now lived cloistered in the back room of the Great Hall of the Sheltered Valley, was absent on an errand to settle a dispute over a sacrificed ewe.

Rak said to Grüt, "You are happy for this wedding?"

Grüt said, "I am happy. We all are happy for this."

Rak said, "Yes, and I am especially happy for my son Stom, and I would do anything to preserve his future as a man." His voice labored, for he carried one end of the stone seat. "Yet our happiness is a balm on our skin to make us unaware of the lawgiver's venomous bite."

Grüt dropped his end of the stone seat, and the thunder echoed throughout the Great Hall of the Sheltered Valley. He said, "What is a venomous bite?"

Rak said, "Before you were born there were tales of a small creature who slithered at the feet of men and bit the skin of men, and the creature was called a serpent, and its bite would send fire through a man's veins, even a man as strong as you, Grüt, and just as the greatest of oxen can be roasted by a patient fire, so the man is consumed by this slow fire in his veins. This is not a glorious death. It is a bad death."

Grüt said, "Why do you say these things?"

Rak said, "The lawgiver has come to rope our jaws when we would roar with rage. We are told to drop our swords and accept payment of food and goods and labor for a death. What is the worth of my corpse, Grüt? Three oxen? A daughter? A season of tilling in a field? What is the price of a man, Grüt? What price would you name for yourself?" And as Rak said this, his countenance darkened.

Grüt readied his bare hands. He said, "The shadow of battle has fallen on you."

Rak said, "I would not fight you, Grüt, but even if I wished to do so, and even if I won, I could not afford the goats and grain it would cost me. Listen to me now. The trumpet blasts from the frozen hall where the glorious dead are gathered, but the lawgiver has packed our ears full with snow so that we might not hear it and join them after a good death. Our grief calls us to be warriors, but our law makes us merchants."

Grüt said, "I do not argue against you, Rak, but I swore my axe to the lawgiver, and my heart follows my blade even into the fiery depths of Heaven. All who wish the lawgiver harm will suffer my rage, for I laid down my law first."

Rak said, "I am not the only man who feels the venomous bite of the lawgiver. The others stay silent only for the moment because their own veins have not been set ablaze. Others stay silent, Grüt, for under the law, they cannot speak the truth out loud. It will not be long until they will be forced to speak one way and act another."

Grüt said, "If every living thing in our land means the lawgiver harm, then every living thing will die by my axe."

Rak turned his back to Grüt and walked out of the Great Hall of the Sheltered Valley, and he said, "I look forward to the wedding tomorrow night." But Rak spoke with slyness, for he intended more than one meaning to his words.

◆ ◆ ◆

Inside the Great Hall of the Valley, orange torchlight filled
the air, and the walls swayed joyously with the bustle of
every man and woman and scurrying child of the Sheltered
Valley. Down the center of the Great Hall of the Valley
stretched the Long Table, which had been hewn from the
side of a marauding ship, and it bowed heavily under the
feast. In heaps and rows there lay shieldfuls of boiled roots,
and logs of bread sopping with butter, and full roasted
hogs, and charred elk, and bowls of browned lamb, and
beside the table, placed like honored guests, sat opened
barrels of iced vodka.

Stom and Sana sat at the head of the Long Table, and
they could not so much as feed each other in the wedding
way because so many people wanted to sing with Stom and
dance with Sana and toast vodka with Stom and give gifts
to Sana. The lawgiver, who remained heavily cloaked as
always, managed to stop everyone for a moment and to
give many good words and blessings to Stom and Sana, and
at these words, the hall burst with cheers of well-wishing,
and the Great Hall of the Valley filled with even more
fervent feasting and drinking and singing and dancing.

During the jubilation, Grüt carried two great goblets of
iced vodka and found the lawgiver sitting in the darkened
corner, and Grüt said, "I have not seen much of you since
the first night you came ashore and I fed you at my own
home and you were very quiet."

The lawgiver said, "We see each other nearly every day,
Grüt."

Grüt said, "Here. Drink. It is very good." And Grüt
drank heavily from his goblet, and then he said, "There is
much joy here tonight, but I fear for your safety."

The lawgiver said, "It sounds odd to hear you speak of
fear, Grüt, but I assure you no one has confronted me or
threatened me." The lawgiver drank from the goblet and
coughed.

Grüt said, "The fear I speak of is a new fear. It is a silent
thing in the hearts of some of the men here among us

tonight, and I think it is even something that they do not say with their words, yet they think it with their minds. True, it does sound odd to speak this way, as I never have before, but because of my concern for you, I must learn the language of fear."

The lawgiver stood and wobbled and put a quick hand to Grüt's arm and said, "Come with me to my room in the back of the Hall and tell me more of your concern for me." And Grüt went, but they did not speak any more of fear. It is said that in the candlelight of the back room of the Great Hall of the Valley, the cloak did drop, and the lawgiver unveiled herself to Grüt.

It is said that Grüt was in awe of this revelation, and that she had him to feel of her milky skin and of her long hair and of her breasts. It is not said whether they lay together, for it is bad luck for a man to guess at such things, but it is said that their passion for one another was like a bonfire in a strong wind.

Stom raised his voice from among the jubilation in the Great Hall of the Valley, and he called for Sana because he could not find her in the crowd. First, Stom called playfully, and then he called with a stern voice. Then with a wavering voice.

Two virgins burst through the doors, and they screamed with terror, and their hands, which trembled in front of their faces, were covered in blood. They said, "Sana lies on the woodpile. She has been raped. She is dead."

The Great Hall of the Valley shook, and the women wailed, and the men cursed terrible things and kicked over barrels of vodka, and Stom ran outside to the dead body of Sana.

Rak stepped atop the far end of the Long Table and said, "I do not see the lawgiver or his protector, but we do not need them now. This is a horror beyond the reign of tribute or law, is it not? The man who did this thing shall be ripped limb from limb by our very hands tonight."

The crowd roared.

The lawgiver came forth from the back room, tugging the cloak close to hide her body, and Grüt followed behind her. She stepped atop the head of the Long Table and said, "I have heard your screaming, and we will act promptly against whoever did this terrible thing, but we will not torture or murder the man responsible, for law still holds the reins of this land."

From the other end of the Long Table, Rak said, "Where was the law to protect poor Sana? Beautiful, soft Sana. What amount of tribute will quell my son's rage and grief? You no longer fool us, lawgiver. I know your secret."

The lawgiver said, "My secret?"

Rak said, "You have made ways for killers to hide among us. Never has a thing like this happened on our land where the killer did not immediately show himself, but your way and your law nurses deception and raises conspirators. How do we know it was not you, lawgiver, who raped and murdered Sana?"

Grüt said, "I tell you now that the lawgiver knew nothing about this horrid thing until this moment."

Rak said, "Even so, this lawgiver has come to a land of warriors, and has cooled our molten blood and would have us lie as helplessly as the corpse of poor Sana. But not anymore. Now our blood burns again, does it not? We will rage. We will have our vengeance."

The crowd roared.

Rak said, "The killer will have certainly fled by now. Gather the five strongest men and the three best trackers and follow his trail through the snow. Grüt should lead this band, for he is the greatest warrior among us, and we can rest certain that no killer will escape him."

Many men raised their voices, asking for Grüt to take them along in pursuit of the killer.

The lawgiver said, "Do not leave, Grüt."

Grüt said, "We must find this killer, and we must move quickly before the winds scatter his trail. And if I find this killer alive, I will bring him back alive, and it will be the lawgiver who will tell us what to do with him. So let this be an end to bickering with words." And Grüt lifted the blunt side of his axe, and smashed the stone seat where

Sana had sat, and the stone split down the middle like firewood.

No man, not even Rak, argued against Grüt.

The lawgiver said, "Please do not leave me, Grüt."

Grüt said to the men who would stay behind, "Will you do any harm to the lawgiver when I am gone?"

The men said, "We will do no harm."

So Grüt said to the lawgiver, "They said they will do you no harm, and we are men who do what we say."

The lawgiver said quietly to Grüt, "Men where I come from do not do as they say. Take me with you."

Grüt said quietly to her, "Then perhaps your laws have made them as they are, but here you have been promised safety, and if you come with me in pursuit of the killer, there is no promise of safety, for there will likely be an ambush or some other dishonest violence." And after he had gathered his men, at the doorway of the Great Hall of the Sheltered Valley, he said to the lawgiver, "I will return very soon."

Under the solstice moon, the group of men had stopped at the top of a mountain that overlooked the Sheltered Valley. Stag Lock knelt in the snow over the tracks they followed, and he had been silent, and the men waited anxiously. Stag Lock said, "Grüt, my eyes may be aging, it is true, but I know tracks well. The ox hooves we follow now through the snow have not been steered by any rider. This ox was running on its own."

Grüt said, "What do you mean?"

Stag Lock said, "I know I sound mad, but do not believe we are following the trail of the killer."

Grüt stood on a pine stump to get a better look down into the Sheltered Valley, and he saw a pillar of black smoke rising from the Great Hall of the Valley. Grüt withdrew his axe from his backstraps, and without looking at the men behind him, he said, "Follow the trail onward, nonetheless. If you find no killer at the end of it, it would be better for you never to return to what will remain of the Sheltered Valley. Now go."

And Grüt ran down the mountain, and like an avalanche, his rage grew, and his rage grew.

Grüt reached the base of the mountain, and the Great Hall of the Valley bloomed with a fire larger than the frame of the Ironbones, and the black smoke rose taller than the fabled cities of the old gods. The Great Hall of the Valley remained standing amidst the roaring flames only on the empty ribs of its wooden frame.

All the men encircled the blaze, and as they stood in the melting snow, they cheered.

Urli pointed and said, "Look, Grüt has returned very soon."

The men turned to see Grüt, who hunched forward like a bull. Grüt let his axe slip from his hands onto the ground, and his heavy breath steamed from his nostrils.

Rak stepped forward and said, "I am sorry, Grüt. I know you are free from blame, but the lawgiver had deceived all of us, and he had deceived you most of all, for law only did harm to all of us. After you had gone, I told all the men that it was the lawgiver who raped and murdered poor Sana. When we called for the lawgiver to come forward, he locked himself inside his room like a coward. So we burned him alive."

Grüt's voice was pained. "You said you would do no harm to the lawgiver when I was gone."

Rak said, "We were forced to lie, for we could not speak and act on the same path until the law was gone. Do you see, Grüt? Only now can we be honest."

Grüt said, "Did she call my name?"

Rak said, "What?" For he was confused at the words Grüt used.

Grüt said, "Did the lawgiver call my name?"

Rak said, "Yes. Your name was called from inside the burning hall many times."

Grüt lifted his axe from the ground, and the leather of its handle creaked under his tightening grip, and the orange light of its blade fell slowly on the faces of all the men. And Grüt realized that he had been wrong in many ways and that Rak was right in one way. He realized that without law men can be honest. And Grüt said, "I will kill everyone."

And the night was long, and Grüt did as he said he would do.

IN WHICH PINCKNEY BENEDICT, KERMIT MOORE, AND I GO A- HUNTING FOR THE BIG MUDDY MONSTER

We were going to hunt Grendel. The reports said that since the late '60s witnesses have been calling it the Big Muddy Monster around here, but we had it otherwise on good authority. Joyce Carol Oates had told Pinckney that John Gardner had told her that he had seen it. First he had heard it howl deep in the woods somewhere one night, and then, one afternoon as he roamed the backroads, he had been forced to rip his wheels to a stop, his bike nearly kicking out from under him. It had crossed the gravel right before his eyes. And it had passed into the shade through some honeysuckle brush, slouching, and the birds hadn't even scattered as it went, but it had been angry regardless— Gardner had just known it. And it stunk. This was while he was teaching down here at Southern Illinois University at Carbondale, and he had told her that seeing it had inspired him to write *Grendel*, and that some time during the writing of it he had begun to believe that it had been the real Grendel, somehow, a calling, a message from the sons of Cain. Never mind that Joyce Carol Oates had said that John Gardner was drunk while he had told her this, and drunk when he had seen it. No such details would interfere with our hunt.

I was packing my late father's Western-style lever-action—a .308 Savage—in his honor. He had gone monster hunting himself back in Kentucky before I was born, but had found that the lunatic baying the farmers complained of were only highway guardrails popping and echoing as they cooled from the sun in the evening (though the chickens that had been found folded inside-out were never explained or accounted for).

Pinckney was packing a tricked-out AR-15 with zombie green stippling on the grip and on the magazines–twelve banana clips arrayed like a zodiac on his belt and tactical vest; free-floating hand guard; IMod stock with cheek welds and a waterproof storage compartment (holding his earbuds and iPod shuffled with Pink Floyd, South African hip-hop, and recordings of his daughter's operas—I don't know about music, but she's good); nickel-coated bolt carrier; aftermarket candy-cane trigger and anti-rotational pin, also zombie green; upgraded barrel, obviously; twenty-decibel suppressor; and about every type of optic and back-up optic and light that there's a rail or swivel for. He named it "The Humanity Department."

Kermit was a deputy in Roanoke, Virginia, and had driven up, just for this hunt, in a tiny little bright-orange fuel-saving two-door, but he was about as big as the car. He also taught self-defense for charity—two canned goods per lesson—but I figured the best lesson was simply to be his size. In the hatchback he had a duffle bag full of Glocks (I never found out how many) and a 12-gauge drum-fed Streetsweeper that he had confiscated and would use as a demonstration piece when he taught classes to other law enforcement folk—just to show them what the bad guys might be hiding in their coolers when you think they're going for a beer. One time he got pulled over with it just sitting there in the back seat. He showed it off to the state trooper, and they got to talking, and they spent the rest of the day just a few miles up at the trooper's uncle's farm blasting surplus garden veggies and talking about the filming difficulties of *Creature from the Black Lagoon*.

But for our hunt, he was packing nothing more than a
BFR .50 Caliber Beowulf, for poetic reasons.

Right before dusk we parked out of the way at the mouth
of an old logging road, and we spent a few minutes cutting
thick-leaved branches and covering the car with the foliage
to hide it from sight. It did not matter whose sight we were
hiding it from. In such endeavors, to get identified was to fail.

We walked through the treeline and kept quiet for a
space. The logging road was a long lawn of grass and
dandelions, and it took us past a couple of small fields
heavy with soy and fenced by trees. The haze of the low
light colored the soybean leaves navy, and they steamed.
When the woods got thicker beside us, we left off the
logging road and hiked in. We wouldn't need trails. Grendel
wouldn't use trails.

The canopy turned night immediately, but we still
spooked away plenty of birds and squirrels hard at work,
all well awake. The air was fatty with the noise of crickets.
We stopped every so often, Kermit and Pinckney scanning
the area and listening. I would begin to do the same but
would get distracted with trying to identify possible poison
ivy. We were all sweating and wiping at mosquitos.

"It was never reported to be seen in exactly the same
place twice," Kermit said. It was the first any of us mentioned
of the fact that we hunted in an entirely arbitrary location.
Any spot was as likely as any other.

I tried to sound grim, overdramatic, saying, "It could
be watching us right now."

"Like Predator," Pinckney said, a little too loud. "That's
what *Predator 2* should have been. It should have been set
at Heorot. Their first hunt on Planet Earth. Beowulf tears
off his arm so he can't go self-nuclear. Then when he tracks
him down to his cave-ship, Grendel's mother is a female
Predator. She makes the male ones look like little twerps.
That's what *Predator 2* should have been."

We all agreed, and we kept moving. Soon we were using
flashlights and stopping more frequently at sounds that

skipped through the brush. We climbed across a creek and got nice and muddy—something that I noted would legitimize our trek—and were working our way up an ascent when we spooked it. It was Grendel for sure. But Kermit caught them in his light, fleeing in slow leaps, white tails flagging us. So we kept on.

And that's when we found the shack.

We swept the perimeter like we had practiced (in person once, a dozen times online, in-game). No one had cared about this shack in years, clearly, but our tactical movement was no less sharp for that fact. Pinckney hacked the kudzu out of the way so we could open the door, and we went inside.

Someone had lived there, once. The skeleton of bedsprings sat near a woodburning stove on its side, though we saw no flue. Coffee tins and swollen car manuals lay scattered on a desk and on some chairs taken from a hospital. All of the more recent cans of beer and party cups were empty and on the floor. An old toaster's guts hung out across some screwdrivers and sockets, and in the corner I pulled back a sheet to uncover a piano.

Pinckney and Kermit high-stepped it over the debris to see it with me, and they both said that it was actually a spinet.

I said, "Oh, yeah," as if I just remembered that. I tried a couple of keys. They were dead.

Pinckney tried some too.

"Just because we can't hear it. . ." Kermit warned. "Be careful who you call for a dance."

Then Pinckney found a key that worked. The twang it made was lonesome, quite unlike what it was surely meant to be. "Listen to that," he said. He kept hitting it. He was hearing some beautiful quality in its sound, in the way it echoed against the corrugated roof, something I wasn't getting. He produced his cell phone—though none of us had signals out here—and he began recording while I beat on the key for him. He was going to use it later for some of his foley projects.

"Quiet," Kermit said.

I stopped.

The string kept humming long after I had let up on the key, but then I realized that some of the sound came from farther off.

Kermit saw something out of the window. "They're singing," he said. "They're crying."

We followed him in a rush outside, and we moved from concealment to cover with the urgency of a raid. But I couldn't hear anything now that we were outside again, and Pinckney didn't seem to either. We just followed Kermit.

At the crest of the ascent, we went prone to avoid the risk of skylining ourselves, and Pinckney scoped ahead with the Humanity Department. It was completely night now, even above the canopy, and we had switched off and gone dark, as black as the leaves.

The little lights beyond the trees made me certain that something was going on in the pasture down there. I could now hear the distant droll of voices. "What is it?" I said.

"I think I see it," Pinckney said.

"What?"

"They have lanterns. Canvas walls." He paused, delighting in something. "It's a hall," he said. "It's charismatics!"

We walked the pasture, which had none of their cars or vans or busses, only horses and buggies, so I guessed that they had met up over at Bald Knob Cross and had come down here on the trails the hard way, to wheel back time just a little, for their own theatrics.

They peeled open the tent flaps and welcomed us into the revival without a word about our guns, though they eyed them. I imagined they thought something at us like, *all they that take the sword shall perish with the sword*. But then I thought back, *he that hath no sword, let him sell his garment and buy one*. But then they thought back, *I will rid evil beasts out of the land, neither shall the sword go through your land*. And I had no comeback for that one.

Inside was an oven full of swaying bodies on folding chairs, kerosene lanterns swaying with them from ropes above, everyone rejoicing in their sweat, which they would not wipe as if it were finally a rainstorm promised them. We were packed in, unable not to touch each other. I stood on my toes to lift my head above the stench of hot body odor that stayed on a roiling boil.

The closer to the front, the more the charismatics were standing or kneeling, arms moving like snakes, heads lolling.

Against the far tent wall, the preacher stood on a storage trunk, reading from a Bible with his eyes closed. "And the Lord said unto him," he said with a light tune, like reciting "Happy Birthday" for an infant. "Therefore whosoever slayeth Cain, vengeance shall be taken on him sevenfold. And the Lord set a mark upon Cain, lest any finding him should kill him."

Beside him, two old women in long skirts beat on the bodies and pickguards of their guitars, but they did not strum, and a third one swept at the grass on the ground beneath them with a broom. They danced. An Army officer in uniform—a full-bird colonel—stood at the front too, tapping a tambourine.

The people moaned. They laughed, and they moaned.

Then the preacher reached out over the heads of the congregation, moving them in an unseen wave like the heads of grain in a wind, and he strained as if trying to touch us all the way at the back, where Pinckney, Kermit, and I still stood. The preacher said, "Have I need of mad men, that ye have brought this fellow to play the mad man in my presence? Shall this fellow come into my house?"

"Yea!" the people said. "Yea!" And some of them spoke with words of bubbles and gargles that I did not understand.

The preacher stepped off his trunk, and he motioned others toward it.

Two men came to him, knelt by the trunk, and began to unlatch it.

A few in the congregation fell to the ground and called out.

And as the men lifted the lid of the trunk, the preacher spoke in tongues himself, saying (as best I could tell), "Ph'nglui mglw'nafh Cthulhu R'lyeh wgah'nagl fhtagn!"

I already knew what was in the trunk before he reached in. They migrated through this area every year, and it would be easy enough to gather a trunkload of them as they crossed the roads. The preacher reached in, and he lifted forth a rattler by its middle.

He spoke the right verses about it, and it whipped around, easily capable of sinking fangs into his arm, but it didn't.

The people moved faster now. They got louder, and they moved faster. The place was a wave pool, too crowded, moving me with them. They babbled. They didn't sing, but I heard the music. I heard the music with them, finally. I was moving to it with them.

Kermit said my name, as if to ask me if I were okay.

But I knew there were more rattlers in that trunk. They shook their tails to our music. I could lift one too. "I'm going up there," I said.

"Don't, Josh," Kermit said. "Don't do it."

"I'm going up there," I said again.

And Pinckney said, "He's going up there!" as if it never occurred to him to try stopping me.

Kermit held my arm, but with all the sweat I slithered right out of his grip. And the preacher waved me forward, and the people waved, and I washed up in the front, at the trunk, and the rattlers smiled up at me.

"Just keep running!" Kermit screamed, hauling me over his shoulders, the tent ablaze behind us, pillars of smoke and pillars of fire roaring with pressurized tank explosions and the wails of the charismatics.

I cried and screamed in high-pitched delirium. My arm was swollen and already turning black from the crook of my elbow out, almost as if the bite had burned me to a blistering crisp.

Pinckney ran ahead with the Humanity Department in one hand—stock in armpit, ready to shoot anything in our path—and in the other hand a thrashing sack that held the rattler that had gotten me. He was screaming.

And Kermit was screaming.

And I was screaming.

Things had gone wrong back there. One after the other, many things had gone very wrong.

We rushed through the lattice of limbs and leaves in the woods, and my arm hurt—like it was being torn off—as I was jostled by Kermit's carrying me while running, but I was in no condition to do my own running. I was lost to terror and prophecy, crying out that we would never make it through this night, that the world itself would come to an end.

The fires behind us caught hold of the treeline. The night sky soaked up its hot bleeding orange. I suppose I was the only one of the three of us watching the scene behind. I saw silhouettes of men and beasts all a-scatter. Large shapes galloped past us faster than we could ever run, but we kept running.

Without stopping, Pinckney shot at something close to his feet and kept running and screaming.

Kermit didn't slow either. I felt us rise over a hill and run down another valley, deep and swamplike. And that's when we stopped.

They stopped screaming, so I did too. Only then could I hear the lunatic baying right in front of us.

The thing rose from the liquid ground, its long head dripping, its thin arms melting and batting at the air as it screamed high and terrible. We stood in a lagoon, a mire, and it stunk like sewage and swine and death. The thing writhed in the middle of that mess before us, the black goo of its skin gleaming in our lights, the ribs of its barrel body shining like rippled shelves. Kermit and Pinckney said nothing, unsure of what to do for it, but it bucked, and shook its drenched mane, and bit at the mud with the flat of its teeth, and it kept screaming at us.

Only I, in delirium, could see the truth of what it was. And in the wild whites of its eyes, and in the blacks of them, it saw me too, and we both knew the sight for what it was. It was the Big Muddy Monster—it was Grendel. It was Humbaba, Minotaur, Behemoth, Fenrir, Cacus of the Eighth Layer, Moloch the Counselor, Nightmare, the

Creature of Frankenstein, Id, Gothmog, Yog Sothoth, Anung Un Rama, and, lo, the Black Horse, whose rider held balances in his hand, whose rider was lost from his mount. It sank in the tar, and I with it, the two of us plates on the scales tipping in turns ever lower under the waves of the mire too slow to perceive, and we could no longer see one another, where we lay crushed in unison under the surface of the earth, as if embraced again by an inexplicable mother, where heat and gravity sang to us, where all things become one in the end, where we could no longer see where either of us began, finally knowing what monsters are for.

THE ALCHEMIST'S BENCH

Akbar Umayl sold antiques and taught karate. He tended to pack so much mysticism into his sales pitches to customers that both businesses soon went under—this is Missouri after all—and he decided to move his new American family back to his home in Tehran. This is not to say that I thought he was a fraud. I didn't. I had bought some nice pieces from him in the past, and I'm sure he could, with a flying kick, knock my glasses through my skull and out my occipital lobe. Professors aren't known for our durability, not even those like the strapping new hire in the department who runs 10-k races for charity and was handed all future sections of my Poe literature course. I didn't raise a fuss over that, as I ought to have. I wanted him to like me, just like I want everyone to like me, for some goddamned reason. So I showed up at Akbar's moving/going-out-of-business sale with a wad of twenties, ready to nab a brag-worthy conversation piece to (a) help him out, (b) console myself for losing my favorite course, and (c) generally enrich the cultural diversity of my living room décor. I wanted to throw a party for the Humanities Department at my house. I had never done so before, and I figured it might turn things around for me.

The final days of the sale took place at Akbar's house, just a few streets over from mine, a suburban neighborhood bordered by a small state park that everyone appreciates and no one visits. The leftovers from his shop and his dojo were consolidated at his place. I poked through the open garage alongside a couple of other neighbors, but nothing there would do at all: some sets of Depression-era glassware, books of coins, Americana relics ranging from restored spinning wheels to a Charlie's Angels pinball machine, bins of once-collectable Christmas ornaments that couldn't possibly hold meaning for Akbar (a Muslim) or myself (a rather open-minded agnostic who tells some people he's Jewish because of his non-practicing father and tells other people he's Buddhist because of his ex-Catholic-turned-hippy mother, and who feels he doesn't know enough science to be an atheist and is, honestly, uninterested in actual religious matters unless he is called upon to be outraged at conservatives). Akbar's garage also had discounted foam gloves used by karate students to hit themselves with. I didn't want those either.

I told Akbar, who stood by sipping afternoon coffee out of a piece of Polish pottery, that I wanted something authentically Iranian.

He took me inside.

His kids sat on the floor of a family room that was boxed up and bare except for the flat-screen in front of them. They watched an age-inappropriate reality show as if trying to soak themselves to maximum density with American pop-culture before their long, dry exodus to the desert.

Akbar's wife cried behind a closed door that we passed. I had met her previously. She was a full-on American blonde, and I wondered whether she mourned leaving her life in Missouri, or feared the life to come in Tehran. I worried that it was both racist and sexist of me to think that Tehran was bad for women, but I couldn't help admiring her dedication. She was going to get on that jet no matter what, for her kids, for him. I envied that. All of my past candidates for soul mate had been scared off by the slightest of annoyances: my supposed snoring, my clumsy love-making, my unpredictable nighttime housecleaning crusades, my inevitable conviction that on the other end of every one of my relationships was a person who secretly hated me, those kinds of things.

Akbar showed me some small tapestries still hanging on the hallway walls. He said they were handwoven to replicate the patterns of prayer rugs used by five different Islamic mystics who had, while alive, spoken with the angels Nakir and Munkar. Then he let me in on a little secret: after I die, Nakir and Munkar will show up at my grave and ask me three questions, and if I get the answers wrong, they will beat me with their giant hammers until Judgment Day.

"I hope the questions aren't about algebra," I said.

He laughed a little. Maybe he got my reference to his people having invented algebra. Or maybe he just felt sorry for me. He turned the little tapestries over to show me how hand-woven the backs were too, but they looked like something I could buy at a kitschy home-goods franchise. At least my guests would think so.

Rather than tell him that, I just said they were too small.

So he led me into the basement.

I waited with one foot on the bottom step while he navigated the dark. He reached about and grunted, and then gave us some dull light from a hanging bulb. He tried another, but it popped and died. He pointed through the shadows toward a tall mosaic vase, a woven basket large enough to hide a body, a marble bust that looked stolen from a museum, some acid-etched metal plates, two huge rugs rolled up and leaning against the near wall.

I shuffled to the basket and lifted the lid. I couldn't tell if it was empty or not, and I wasn't about to reach down into the dark.

Akbar said he was considering destroying it along with everything else down here, but that I could talk him out of it.

I asked him why he would want to destroy them.

He told me that the basket had been cursed and subsequently spit upon by a shepherd who had placed a lamb in there and had found, to his dismay, that the lamb had immediately disappeared. This had happened a few hundred years ago, he said.

"Then why not sell it to the mafia?" I said. "They'd pay a lot for a garbage disposal like that."

He made no attempt to laugh that time. He seemed, perhaps, offended. "These relics would be better off destroyed than poorly possessed," he said. "People don't appreciate the same kinds of things here."

By *people*, he meant Americans. I felt a little guilty, though I wasn't exactly sure about what, so I feigned interest in a bench against the far wall. I asked about it and went nearer to inspect it.

"I am afraid to destroy that piece," he said. "The fire I put to it might burn the world."

I wasn't going to fall for those kinds of story-time sales gimmicks, but I ran my hand along the seat of the bench, and the dark lighting was no illusion: its wood had been worn to a rich black with the age of decades, maybe centuries. The legs curved out at low, sweeping angles. Letters of the Persian alphabet had been hand-carved with such skill that I could run my finger in the grooves like a paintbrush. It could have been the seat of a sheik or of a peasant, worth a million dollars, or snatched by me for a hundred. It was perfect.

"How much?" I said.

"Do not sit on it," he said. "It is unsafe."

I hadn't thought to sit on it until he said not to, and I knew that my suddenly wanting to sit on it made me the kind of sucker salesmen love, but I sat on it anyway. I smiled and showed my hands like a magician. "Looks like I survived," I said. "So how much?"

"It is cursed," he said. "And priceless."

"How about a hundred dollars?" I had meant my first offer to be fifty, but I knew the exact nook by the window in my house where I would set it, and I knew what books I would put on one end, and I could just see that new professor who took my favorite classes from me sitting on the other end with his snifter of bourbon, reaching down to rub the lettering and admire the craftsmanship, wondering whether he would be able get one for himself—which he wouldn't—while the other professors would gather around me and ask about it. We'd all admire it together, and I would explain the kinds of teachings Akbar had just shared with me about the afterlife beliefs of his people. Then I would tell them how we had talked about the mathematics of *al-jabr*, and how much I miss Akbar already, and that would lead into a discussion of the current politics of Tehran, which I would research before the guests showed up. This bench was perfect.

Akbar said, "If you promise to keep it hidden away, and to leave nothing on it, and never to sell it, and not to sit on it for very long, and to forget that I was the man who sold it to you. . ."

Here it came. He was going to ask five hundred, maybe eight. I could swing three hundred, tops.

He said, "Then I will sell it to you for one dollar."

"One dollar?" I said. "What's the catch?"

He shrugged. "It is cursed."

"Then I'll take it."

Later that evening I attended the refreshments session that followed each event in our university's Arts and Letters Lecture Series. While most of the others stood holding clear plastic cups half-filled with light beer or cheap chardonnay in the midst of catering tables that circled them like covered wagons, I stayed on the edges of the gathering nibbling little cubes of cheese from a napkin and staying near my bottle of water—alcohol tended toward adverse effects with me—and trying to glean what the lecture had included. I had been unable to bring myself to actually attend because the speaker was that new professor. His subject had been, of course, Poe. I had simply waited in one of the stalls of the bathroom until the reception began.

I spotted a philosophy professor carefully considering the cocktail weenies before him, and whether he should add them to his plate of cauliflower and carrots. I said, "What struck you most about the lecture?"

"The doppelganger in all his stories," he said. And then, while still leering at the weenies, he said, "Fascinating."

I was aghast. Six years ago, when I had been the featured lecturer—also discussing the works of Poe—I had mentioned that Poe's ideas could never divorce themselves from the fear of the doppelganger, whether consciously as in "The Imp of the Perverse," or unconsciously as in "The Tell-Tale Heart." I had gone even further to posit that Poe was pre-doppelganger for many writers to come.

"Tell me more," I said to the philosopher. "What fascinated you about it."

He said, "I guess the idea of Poe's influence as pre-doppelganger."

As nonchalantly as possible, despite my small quake of indignation, I mentioned, "I remember pointing out something extremely similar when I gave the lecture a little while back."

"Curious," he said, finally deciding to gather a line of weenies between a pair of tongs and roll them onto his plate. "They sprung for the name brand ones. They say the others are the same, but they're not."

I looked around. Everyone chatted like everything was fine. No one was noticing that this new professor was a plagiarist—my plagiarist. "Did he at least mention Borges?" I asked.

"What?"

"Did he mention Borges? Or did he just default to Lovecraft?"

The philosopher looked at me quizzically, grinding away at a fat mouthful of sausage meat, and said sloppily, "Did you not even go to it?"

I made some vague comment and excused myself as if in the non-committal way one leaves for the bathroom meaning to return. My mistake before fleeing the event was looking back at the new professor, who, mid-conversation with a dozen other faculty members—half of whom wanted to date him—looked up and made eye-contact with me. If I were a handsomer version of myself, I'd be him.

I spent the remainder of that evening in a manic rearrangement of my living room furniture around the ancient Iranian bench, and then giving up and moving the bench to different rooms, and then returning to where I had placed it to begin with.

I finally got it looking right when I realized my difficulty was merely a matter of lighting. I angled the lamps so as to re-create some of the half-lit shadows of Akbar's basement. And to complete the scene, I set on one end of the bench my 1952 edition of *The Aleph and Other Stories,* crudely signed, dated, and noted by the author: "*Jorge Luis Borges, 1977, Nadie en el espejo.*" It meant, *No one in the mirror.* I had had it officially authenticated by an expert and had been told that its uniqueness was due in large part to the fact that, at the time of that inscription, Borges had already gone blind.

Before closing my own eyes for a fitful night's sleep, just before midnight, I sent out a mass e-mail invitation to everyone in the Humanities Department for a party at my house at the end of that week, assuring them that no RSVP would be necessary since there would be plenty of food, music, and illuminating conversation about unique ideas—I italicized that last adjective for a certain someone—to go around for all who show up. I also said I would provide free liquor.

The next morning, I stumbled around the kitchen to prepare my freshly ground coffee, then balanced the full mug and blew on the steaming black surface as I went to the living room to admire the bench, and that's when I noticed a second book under the signed Borges edition. I remembered specifically placing only the one book there before I retired to bed, but the first thing I did was doubt my memory. So I lifted *The Aleph* to see what book I must have lain under it, and I saw another copy of *The Aleph.*

Then I no longer doubted my memory. I possessed no other copy of that book, nor had I ever come across another that looked so much like my 1952 edition. I set my coffee mug down on the bench to free my hands for inspecting this second book further. And, upon opening its cover, I found a duplicate—down to the subtlest curve of each letter—of the unique inscription: "*Jorge Luis Borges, 1977, Nadie en el espejo.*"

I had been assured that experts had never seen a second of this inscription, as I was seeing now.

I checked for anything else unique. I flipped inside the book to a page near the middle that had once been folded in half. I found it, so I compared it to the original book, and they both held the same crease on the same page. I flipped through both again, finding a blotted brown stain across a page in one, finding the same stain in the other. The blotch had faint branches at its edges, like the tips of a snowflake, where some drop of tea had long-ago splashed. Down to the tiniest fractal, the patterns were identical.

I realized what this meant. My stomach turned a cold sour, and I could feel my pulse in my ears. I looked around me for pranksters to jump out with cameras in their hands and laugh, or for a clue such as an unlatched window showing where someone had snuck in, left this forged duplicate under the original, and left. But I found nothing to support the theories of prank or hoax, just as my adrenal system had already intuited. And I had to acknowledge that no one cared enough about me to try such a thing. I was alone in this miraculous discovery. This was no forged duplicate by any person. The bench had done it.

I immediately took my coffee off of the seat and put it on a table elsewhere, fearing now to drink it.

Returning to the two books lying side-by-side on the bench, I couldn't recall which was the original—the one on the left or the right. And like wafts of steam, the realizations hit softly again and again: I had merely assumed the book on top had been the original. If they were exactly the same, neither was the original. Or, that is to say, they both were. And if this bench could duplicate an item with absolute exactness, I could use it to duplicate something far more valuable.

I soon returned from the bank with a small stack of hundred-dollar bills. It amounted only to four thousand; I didn't have as much in savings as I should have. But that was about to change.

I set the stack of cash in the middle of the bench and waited. An hour elapsed, and other than my getting new coffee in the kitchen while keeping a steady watch over the bench, nothing happened.

I decided that the bench couldn't do its magic while being watched, so I took some time away, long enough to call into work to lie about an emergency concerning my (non-existent) significant other—for whom I even made up the name Naaji—canceling all my classes for the day. Then I wandered the house, trying to give the bench some privacy.

A half-hour later, nothing changed. Without lifting the cash off the bench, I flipped through the bills to give them a rough count, still finding only forty.

So I put myself on a steady schedule of watching the bench for an hour, and walking away to wander the house for an hour. I spent much of the time considering what else I could duplicate that would benefit me more than cash, coming to the same conclusion each time that cash would be best. To further pass the time, I tried without a calculator to determine how many doublings of my original four-thousand dollars I would need to become a millionaire. Eight, I figured, and not many more to be a billionaire. The flocking attention given to the new plagiarist professor would scatter from him and roost at my arms the moment I walked through the doors at the next lecture, which would be held in the new auditorium that had my name graven over the entrance. My colleagues would be endowed by me. My soul mates would stand in line. But I knew in getting there I would have some troubles with taxation, so I ran through some ideas on money laundering, and finally decided that I would pay someone else to work all that out for me.

I drank pomegranate juice and did nothing else than watch the bench, and think about the bench, and watch it some more.

But when the sun set, and still nothing had happened, I worried that the bench could duplicate only one item per owner, or maybe only one item per century, and I felt the sharp regret of ignoring Akbar's warning that the bench was cursed. The curse, it seemed, lay not in the bench but in the mind of the owner. If tomorrow was a duplication of today, and the next day a duplication of that, I would soon go mad.

Because I forced myself to stay away from the bench all night—not to even sneak the quickest peek—I paced the floor of my bedroom and got no sleep. At sunrise, I rushed back to the bench.

And on the bench, lo and behold, sat two stacks of cash.

I jumped with my hands in the air and cheered in a whisper—I couldn't have the neighbors hearing me. I could let no one find out what I had.

Gruesome thoughts of what I would need to do with Akbar and his family came to my mind but quickly flew away. They would be in Tehran by now. They were out of the picture. The bench was my secret, mine alone.

And now I had discovered the secret to its operation: I had to leave the item to be duplicated overnight.

I removed the identical lead-colored rubber bands from both stacks, sat on the floor in front of the bench, and counted out every hundred-dollar bill in front of me, one by one, keeping the bills from each stack with their own kind, to my left and to my right.

I now had eight thousand dollars. Tomorrow morning I would have sixteen. The next morning would be thirty-two, and so on for the rest of my life.

But then I picked up the first two bills from each of the stacks—left and right—and I realized the bad news, a fact that would have come naturally to the mind of any seasoned criminal—whether his crimes were occult or otherwise. The serial numbers were exactly the same.

I mindlessly called the campus to cancel what remained of my classes for the week, not even bothering with an excuse. Too much was on my mind. I needed a solution for the bench.

Duplicating more high-priced collectors' items—like the Borges book—would be too inefficient, perhaps not resulting in real money for years.

Casino chips made the most sense, at least immediately. The highway signs boasted of casinos being no farther than an hour's drive in every cardinal direction. I could easily cash in the four grand for chips, return here to stack them in a neat pyramid on the bench, duplicate them overnight, and return to cash out eight grand.

But I knew what would happen. The security guards would mark me like imperial spear-holders spotting a crooked little magician approaching the throne of a pharaoh. They would let me try to cash out, watching me the whole time, and even if I had the nerve to follow through under their gaze, even if they didn't have little electronic identifiers in each chip, I would give myself away somehow. They would ask me to step into the back room, and I would be too frightened to resist, and I would admit everything. Would they believe me? Would it matter?

I would need to find a better way to duplicate wealth.

Diamonds seemed to make some sense, but an economics prof on campus had once told me about their inflated retails scams, and I doubted that I would hold up under scrutiny any better if I walked up to a jeweler with a shoebox full of identical diamond rings and he called the cops.

Pure gold was the only solution. Un-minted bars would be best, but I would be able to melt them down myself on my gas stove if I had to. Everything else in the modern world was numbered and labeled and tracked and dated and accounted for. Everything was too unique. But a slice of pure gold from Fort Knox was the same as a slice of pure gold from King Tut. A single, pure ingot was one with all the pure gold on the planet. Gold in the hand was the exact same as gold in any fairy tale. Gold was its own archetype. Only gold could be duplicated and remain true. So only gold was really true.

It took me most of the day following flawed GPS guidance from one shop to another before I finally found a place still in business that claimed to allow not just cash for gold but also the reverse. The building looked new: a small, stucco construction the color of pottery and nearly the size. The sign let me know that closing time was minutes away.

Inside, a kid with a goatee sat behind the glass counter, deftly tickling the buttons on a video-game controller, watching the magic he worked on the screen. He must have been cheating. The car he controlled kept hitting a ramp on a rooftop, flying over the streetlamps, and ever-so-closely failing to land on the next rooftop, before the whole scene reset, and he tried again, and again. I stood near the counter and made throaty sounds ostentatiously like a valued customer, waiting for him to fetch his boss.

He duplicated his car stunts endlessly and without success.

"Is the owner here?" I finally asked.

"You got him," the kid said. "What can I do for you?"

I looked for any sign that he was fucking with me, but he was too busy with the game to have tried.

I said, "I need to buy gold. A lot of it. In a single un-minted bar."

"What for?" the kid said.

"What for?" I thought about how I wanted to answer that. Never before that moment had I been forced to resist ripping a power cord out of a wall and whipping someone with it. I said, "What do you care what I need it for?"

"If I'm going to be your hook-up, I want to be convinced."

"Convinced of what?"

"That it's worth the effort."

"I have a lot of cash," I said. "Is that not enough these days?"

"Not really," he said. "It'll take me some time to score. I might have to cast it myself. Tomorrow afternoon at the fastest. So what if I do all that and you never show back up?"

"You're worried about wasting time?" I said.

He paused his video game and looked away at his profound thoughts. "It's the only thing we lose that we can't buy back."

"That's not the only thing you could lose," I said, sounding like I did when correcting my soft-brained students, simultaneously disappointed and ominous.

"You threatening me?" He opened his ironic green cardigan to show me the pistol he wore in a shoulder holster. "Because I'll waste you right now. I don't even care."

If I had merely tested this scenario out in my head, as I had with the casino, this moment would have concluded with my fleeing from the shop and driving away in urine-soaked pants. At least that would have been my hypothesis. But I would have been wrong. Instead, what I observed was that I seemed made out of minerals. I felt nothing except a desire to get what I came for and to return to my bench. I couldn't tell what had already begun changing in me, but something had.

I told him, "I could lose my life, sure, as could you. But we could also lose our sanity. Our identity. Our love for something. Our love for all things. There is much one could lose, much, much more than time."

"I got you," he said. He closed his cardigan and nodded. "True that. True that."

I slapped the four-thousand dollars in cash on the glass countertop and said, "And here's how you'll know I'll be back tomorrow."

He pulled the cash out of sight without counting it. "Yeah, okay," he said. "But how do you know I'll be here?"

"Do you believe in black magic?" I said.

I had his attention. He had ceased to be safely amused by me at some point in our discussion.

He said, "What kind of black magic?"

"The kind that's real. The kind that drives a guy like me to drive around the state all day until he can buy unmarked gold from a guy like you."

He watched me, slow to answer. He eventually said, "I guess so."

"Then that's how I know you'll have my gold tomorrow afternoon."

That evening, as proud of myself as I had initially been, I dismantled my house in a panic. The bench was there as I had left it—everything was as I had left it—but I had nothing to duplicate until I could get my gold the following day. A whole night would be wasted, unless I could find something of value to duplicate. I had to have owned something that would use a night of duplication wisely.

I ripped apart my bedroom, every dresser drawer, every box in the back of my closet, finding nothing more valuable than a few old coins and a geode. I tore apart the extra bedroom I used as an office, realizing how completely worthless every modern implement was: printer cartridges, cell-phone charging stations, laptops, back-up hard-drives, all of it top-dollar name-brand, and all of it useless junk. Nothing in my world had any value of its own.

Finally, deep in the back of a kitchen cabinet, I found a set of my grandmother's silverware. It was a weak substitute for gold, but I was the closest substitute I had.

I stacked all the silverware pieces on the bench, breathed with sane relief, and then locked myself away for the rest of the night.

The next morning—after very little sleep, if time enough for just one nightmare counted as sleep—I had double the amount of silverware, even though some had fallen onto the floor. That must have happened after duplication. I wasted no time with exploring such wonders, however. Instead, I scooped all the silverware into a large pot, set it on the stove over a gas burner on high, and drove off to collect my gold.

❖   ❖   ❖

That evening I returned to a foul-smelling house, having acquired a pathetic little turd of a gold bar.

I checked the stovetop to find that the silver had not melted all day but instead passed wisps of weird gas throughout the house. I switched off the burner and gave up on it.

Back at the shop, the kid had seemed extraordinarily concerned that I understood how little my four thousand could actually procure. He had re-weighed everything for me in person, had taken me through several Websites on current market values, had proved that he erred to my benefit by three grams. He had apologized the whole time.

I was perhaps disappointed, but I would not let my mind boil over. I knew it would be enough gold to get started, enough to double, quadruple, octuple, sexdecuple, and so on.

I set it on the bench that night, turned off all the lights in the house except the softly glowing lamp on the floor beside me that was built inside a block of Himalayan salt—an old gift from my mom—and I sat amid my pillows and blankets cross-legged like an Old-Testament herdsman, and drank straight from a bottle of liquor distilled from figs, called *boukha*—an old gift from my dad. I wondered how either of my parents, both of whom seemed awful at their own relationship, managed to keep the other from leaving all those years. With regularity around this part of the season—the first of the winter frosts—one or the other would ask, with all the callousness that only parents find acceptable, what was wrong with me and why I always seemed to sabotage my relationships and end up alone. As many times as I had answered their clueless and outdated questions, I had only started wondering the same thing myself in recent years. I knew I would have trouble sleeping without the *boukha*. I was desperate for sleep, for this plan to finally work, for everything in my life to work.

I awoke late in the morning sprawled out with puke dried to the side of my face. I hurt from guts to brains with a

hangover, and I had trouble seeing with all the light shining
in through the closed blinds. My glasses cut into my back,
and I retrieved them painfully, getting a smear of my own
blood across my palm and finding the frames snapped in
half. I felt for the bottle of *boukha* nearby and finished the
last two swigs, immediately feeling the buzz from the hair
of the dog that bit me, immediately feeling better.

I sat up to inspect the bench. Where there had been one
little bar of gold the evening before, now there sat two.

This would finally work. I would be well off in a week,
rich in a month, and, in a year, as wealthy as a god.

I spent the day nursing my hangover and deciding not
to drink that night even if it meant losing sleep again. I
couldn't trust myself to start drinking the hard stuff now
that I saw how absolutely steam-rolled I had let myself
get. I needed to keep watch on my bench.

That night, still on the pallet in front of the bench, I tried
not to look toward the seat where the two bars of gold
would turn into four. I wondered whether the duplicates
popped suddenly into existence at 12:01 Central Standard
Time, or whether they faded slowly into existence, or
whether Nakir and Munkar snuck them into the house
like Santa with presents. It seemed a sin to watch the
duplication happen, or maybe watching would have broken
the magic, so I looked away all night. I might have slept an
hour, maybe less. Part of what kept me awake was a new
worry: since this bench was cursed and priceless as Akbar
had warned, what else was true? Would Nakir and Munkar
truly visit my grave after death? If I could not answer their
questions, would they beat me with giant hammers until
Judgment Day? That which seemed so silly to me previously
was now genuine dread across the long hours of that
sleepless night.

At daybreak, I allowed myself to look at the seat of the
bench. Where two bars of gold had sat the evening before,
now there sat three.

I screamed.

Then, angry at myself for making noise that neighbors could hear, I cried, and I snotted along the sleeves of my shirt, which I had not changed in—how many days had it been since I had changed my clothes, or showered? I did not care.

Why were there only three bars of gold and not four? It couldn't have been a matter of separate items. The book made of many pages had been duplicated down to every last page. The stack of cash had duplicated entirely, the same with the pile of silverware. I had stacked the two gold bars, one on top of the other, yet there sat one more bar beside them rather than two more.

I held them, inspected them, put them back, inspected them again, set them back, left the room, then returned and inspected them again, set them back again, crying the whole time.

It was too much for me. I left the house, went to a liquor store where I blindly grabbed half a cartful of bottles of the hard stuff, paid out hundreds of dollars for it all— with the cash of duplicated serial numbers—and was already drinking from of one of the bottles by the time I pulled back into my driveway and stumbled from my car, not caring to shut the driver-side door.

Inside, the three gold bars continued being only three. But the liquor had helped me stop crying. The bottle I sipped from was some cheap imitation of my father's *boukha*. That's how I realized the solution: the bench could not copy a copy. The real-world original could produce an exact duplicate, but that exact duplicate—being from some other dimension, or some other quantum possibility, or from Hell—that one could not produce another.

Maybe I was wrong. Maybe each item could duplicate only once, and maybe it didn't matter whether it had been the real-world original. I wasn't sure.

I had a gut feeling about the former hypothesis, but I couldn't rule out the latter just yet. It was otherwise impossible to tell which of the three gold bars had been the real-world original, and which was the second duplicate, and which was the third, especially not now that I had rearranged them, but I had to know. Sipping the fig liquor and drawing diagrams on printer paper—then needing more space and drawing diagrams on the living-room walls—I worked out dozens of ways to run tests. It took the whole day to figure out how to reduce the wasted nights differentiating the original gold bar from the second duplicate, but solid answers came after hours of research on Game Theory, especially the Monty Hall "choose a door" probability problem.

But since I was dedicating myself to testing the bench to further understand its physics—or was it *metaphysics*? Once a paranormal phenomenon revealed itself to be real, would it be downgraded to mere *physics*? Did ancient magicians, if successful, practice mere chemistry?—I realized that I should test something more insightful than a mere gold bar, something infinitely more complex. I should test a living being.

And why start with just a spider, or toad, or cat? Why not a large mammal?

Then I realized what a fool I had been.

I laughed at myself aloud, not fearing to alert the neighbors. What a fool I had been! I drank more to celebrate my insight.

I had been trying to duplicate mere gold. The price of gold per ounce was high indeed, but what was that compared to the price of the exact right match for a kidney? How much gold could buy the perfect liver for a transplant? Bone marrow, skin grafts, non-mangled limbs for reattachment—a single body was worth more than its weight in gold.

And sheer value wasn't all, of course. The implications were now vaster than wealth. Stem cell research, cloning, gene therapy—civilization bent all its will toward fending off death, toward the preservation of life, and all its mighty achievements would shrink under the shadow of that which I could produce in a single night. With a coven of chemists around me, I could cure genetic disease in a week, cure cancer in a month, and in a year, overtake death itself.

In one hand I had limitless gold, and in the other, immortality.

And maybe, just maybe, something more could be gained by duplicating a human than eternal life. Human history has watched countless men and women sacrifice both wealth and life for one thing above all. Maybe I could use the bench to duplicate that too. Maybe an immortal life didn't have to be lived alone.

To begin, all I needed was a human test subject.

Then someone knocked on the door.

It was night. I had no idea who it could be, but there were voices, many of them. They were—it sounded like—they were laughing. Why were they laughing?

I threw open the door. Half a dozen members of the Humanities Department stood on my front porch, wearing coats, huddling from the cold. Some had foil-covered party trays; others had store-bought bags of chips. One of them said, "It's still on, right?"

With music blasting, lighting low, snacks abundant, a dozen bottles of liquor generously opened and free for the pouring, my party quickly mimicked everything that a party was supposed to be. But everyone seemed uneasy. They acted polite enough, and said nice things about my house and décor, but they talked softly among each other and kept gathering in small groups away from me.

I had splashed some cologne on quickly, so it wasn't my stench. I looked rough, surely, but I had swept up my pallet from the floor and acted like everything was normal. Maybe it was because I was a tad drunker than everyone else. They had been at work all day, while I had been sipping ambrosia and unlocking the mysteries of the universe.

Keeping to the living room as often as I could, I tried to get them to relax. I started dancing to an old song that came on from Kid Creole and the Coconuts, taking heavy swigs of liquor between bouts of flailing my elbows, shaking my butt side to side, and saying "yeah" a lot. I danced like a sheik, like a pharaoh.

That new professor seemed to get a kick out of watching me dance by my bench, so I motioned for him to come closer. "I want to show you something," I said. "Have a seat."

He yelled for me to repeat myself over the music.

So I yelled for him to have a seat.

He did.

"Comfortable?"

He admired the bench beneath him and traced the Persian writing just as I had done. "Nice piece," he said. "Where'd it come from?"

"There's no other like it," I said. "Do you think you could sleep on it?"

"No, too small." He held the sides and tested his weight. "It'd be pretty uncomfortable."

I took a heavy swig and then handed the bottle to him. He didn't want it, but I forced him to drink, holding the bottle so that he had to sputter and gulp. I said, "A few more of those, and that bench might as well be a king-sized bed. Sleep like the dead."

"Say what?" he said under all the noise.

I tried forcing him to drink again, but he struggled back this time. I screamed, "Sleep like the dead!"

But someone had just killed the music right before I said it. I had screamed in a silent house. Everyone was watching me, as still as statues.

"What?" I asked them. "What's the problem?" I took the bottle back and drank some more to show them that we were all just having a good time. "See?" I drank again and danced in the silence. I danced the dance of kings, to the sound of their tombs, to the sound of great tomorrows rolling out before me, the glorious silence.

Some of them excused themselves as they left, but most of them just left. I tugged on the arm of that new professor, begging him to stay, just a few minutes more, promising him that I could show him something amazing, but I could hear how slurry and vague I sounded.

He kept apologizing to me as he pulled away, telling me that he wasn't interested.

I scoffed. He thought I wanted his interest. I scoffed again, and then realized that I had.

He was the last one out, locking the door from the inside out of courtesy before shutting it behind himself. I sulked there and drank some more. I remember slumping on the bench to prove to myself that he could have indeed slept on it. But a waft of dizziness hit me, as if the world rolled the wrong way. It was followed by quick drowsiness, and, after that, all was blank.

The unmistakable sound of squealing tires—and then of speeding away in a panic—from my driveway wakes me. It is morning. My front door is wide open. My joints ache worse even than my head, and my ribs feel as though I slept with an anvil on my chest. I sit up and see. I had passed out on the bench, overnight.

I rush to the window and catch a glimpse of my car turning the corner at the far end of the road. The figure at my wheel could be a simple car thief, some stranger noticing the careless and vulnerable state of my car.

But, for all I saw, that figure could have been me. The other me could have awoken, found the original me lying below, and then fled in a panic.

It could have been the panic of an unholy being looking down to see me, the original, the creator. Or it could have been the panic of a creator. What if I am the duplicate?

I lock the door. I rush to the kitchen and arm myself with two steak knives, one in each hand, identical, both looking at me like dim mirrors. I need to be ready to kill the other me. A murder conviction would be no worry. Even if they found the remains of the body, its DNA would prove to be merely my own.

But would the other me think the same way? That one might be out there acquiring a gun right now, for we both know we don't have one here in the house. Would I do that? Would I have gone to get a gun? We know exactly where to go to buy one without any waiting-period hassle. The other me went to the kid's shop.

No, maybe we are panicking and just need to calm down. We can meet back up with cooler heads and talk it out, even find a way to use this blunder to great advantage. We could even find a way to live in a miraculous harmony, more harmonious than any two people have ever lived, alone nevermore.

And after we talk it out, after the other me feels safe, that's when I will strike. I will go straight for the throat. I will have to. There is no way around it. The other me will know that I need to be killed sooner or later, and I know that the other me knows it.

The only difference between us is that the other me has a head-start on acquiring better weaponry. I have no knowledge or skill that the other me doesn't also have. The other me has every advantage. No matter what I do, I will lose. I will die today. My world is at an end. And maybe that is just as well, since I am in all likelihood the mere copy. Maybe I always was.

The only element to my advantage is that I still possess the bench.

If my world is at an end, I will make it an end that is, for the first time on the planet, unique.

I hoist the bench over my shoulder, and, with the two knives at my belt, I haul it out of the house, out of the neighborhood, deep into the state park at the edge of town. I ignore the trails and hike into the most remote pack of trees in the bottom of a small valley, nestling low among the damp stones. The hills on either side hide me from discovery. Here, I am alone in the absolute.

Hours passed in getting to this spot, and I feel ill. I drink from a stagnant pool and rest. Squirrels rustle the leaves. I am surrounded by animal, mineral, and vegetable, all of which I can duplicate.

I can duplicate everything.

The other me has probably made it back to the house and has begun hunting me by now, but it will be no use. The other me won't find me; no one will, not until tomorrow, not until it is too late.

I sit before the bench, and I already grow cold though the sun has not yet set.

I think about what I am about to do just one more time, just to make sure I have the resolve. Then I do it: I lift the bench, turn it upside down, and I press the seat down onto the ground. Sitting on the bench now is the entire earth.

Then I lie back onto the cold leaves, their moisture seeping into my clothes. I watch through the fracturing branches the vast sky that lies under the bench, feeling beneath myself the whole hard planet, a thing that has been the only one of its kind for so long, alone in the universe for so long, knowing that although I will not survive the cold of tonight, my death will herald a collision like none other, for tomorrow will welcome a whole new world.

SMALL DEAD MONKEY

"...discovery of a small dead monkey in a back garden at Broadmoor, California, early in the morning of 26 October 1956 by Mrs. Faye Swanson. The 4 by 4-inch post holding her clothes-line had been splintered, presumably when struck by the falling creature. It was theorized that the monkey had fallen from a plane, but an airport spokesman said no planes had been carrying monkeys that night..."
—*San Francisco Chronicle*, 27 October 1956

She is enthralled at how his little paws curl, frozen in a grasp as if for some lost toy, some absent parental finger. Infants hold this way: their little hands clamp, taut muscles under pudding-soft skin, as if their need for a mother never to leave them channels strength into their small bodies, channels down strength like bolts of lightning, those sudden columns of God, channels down strength in direct plummets from the strange halls of Heaven.

"Faye?"

"Kitchen."

"Hello to you, too. What's all this?"

"Leftovers in the oven."

"What's all this? Out in the yard."

"They're taking photos of my monkey."

"In the garden? They're taking photos?"

"I think it was only a baby."

"Did they talk to you?"

"It was a boy."

"Did they talk to you?"

"Yes."

"I'm going to go talk to them. What's all this about a monkey?"

"If I held three tomatoes in my hands, I could have been holding him. He's that small."

Their Chevy was a steam engine, the radiator sucking two gallons of water at a time in Evansville, then St. Louis, then Kansas City, then north of Topeka, then so on and so on into the west. Faye wanted to wear her big sunglasses the entire way, even at night, and Tim said that he could always tell the difference between when she rested her eyes and when she slept. Her bottom lip pouted when she slept.

Faye finger-tapped AM tunes onto her belly and propped her bare feet out of the passenger window and wiggled her piggies through hundreds and hundreds of miles of wind. Angels run this way.

Tim said that the first big bug to splatter into her foot would make her scream bloody murder. A sharp one hit like yellow yolk, and she screamed bloody murder. He laughed. She laughed. He needed to stop making her laugh because she had to pee—the baby was making her have to pee a lot more.

San Francisco—Faye breathed in through the mouth. She licked the air—ah, San Francisco, a fresh place at the end of the earth before the globe turns on itself and begins again. She and Tim decided that they would begin again. They would start a new calendar, just a few unmentioned months off from nine, and in a year or two the family back home would never be able to tell the difference, and the air back in Kentucky, inside her father's house, would taste far less bitter. Here, the air had been salted by the great cosmic Cook from His golden kitchen—salted by the Master of ingredients who, unlike Faye, never drops a thing.

For my own part I would as soon be descended from that heroic little monkey. . .as from a savage who delights to torture his enemies, offers up bloody sacrifices, practices infanticide without remorse, treats his wives like slaves, knows no decency, and is haunted by the grossest superstitions.

—Charles Darwin, *The Descent of Man*

Tim seemed like the most decent of men. Sure he wanted to drive her out to the hill overlooking his campus, cut the headlights, and descend onto her just like the high school boys wanted to. But she allowed Tim to because he talked rationally at her. She surrendered the sonnets of her some-day shining knight—off to the clouds with them—because Tim could tell her things such as why her father practiced the kind of faith he did, or, as Tim put it, why her father succumbed to the ever-present lure of ancient irrationality. He required it like a junkie, Tim would say, the opiate of the masses. She learned that although her father was a savage of sorts, he was surely not an evil man because evil, again, was a fabrication of his system, a system of superstitions.

After meeting Tim—being with Tim—little things changed. Dinners with her father changed:

"More."

"More of what?"

"Girl, I said more."

"Yes, sir, but more what?"

"Faye, are you testing out your Eve tongue? Do I need to mention again the old forked tongue of women?"

"I can't know for certain what your needs are, so I can't truthfully answer that question, and it is wrong for me to speak untruthfully. Shouldn't we all say just what we mean? Such as what you were asking more of?"

"Potatoes."

"Yes, sir. They are. Baked in orange juice, wrapped in tin foil, just as you prefer." She felt like Tim's Socrates. She was forcing her father to be obvious, to unveil.

"I mean, *pass* the potatoes."

"Yes, sir." And with that, she won.

And she won again, and again, small pebbles of a mountain victory. Tim kept speaking through her week after week, and the balance of control slid grain by grain to her side of the house. Surely a father of such great faith could appreciate the movement of a mountain at the scale of a mustard seed.

Or perhaps he simply appreciated the patience of mountains.

For how else could he have known if he had not been waiting for it—suspecting, but biding his time? How had he known she had been crying in the bathroom that day? How had he known that she had tossed the calendar and the pen to the tile floor and held, trembling, the unblemished pad of cotton? It was so small in her hands. How had he known exactly when—exactly when—to strike at her?

"Tim, I think I have to keep him. I have to. Go back out there and tell them they can't take him."

"It really is a monkey. Can you believe that? An actual monkey."

"Tell them they can't."

"Did you see what it did to the clothesline? The little thing must have been frozen like a rock. Or frozen inside a chunk of ice—now that might make sense. From an airplane."

"Tell those men that I am keeping him."

"Keeping him? Surely we should leave it to them. The officials, honey. You don't have any idea if it's diseased or not. You have to think about your health first."

"Tim, you let them take my baby. They will not take him too."

Faye kneels in the dry dirt. The nape of her neck can feel Tim, back there at a distance, whispering and exchanging bewildered, excusing looks with the photographers from the *San Francisco Chronicle*. He is most likely exchanging cash as well since their engines start back up and pull away with little more fuss. A splinter from that broken cross of a clothesline stabs into the skin of Faye's knee, but it doesn't matter if she bleeds just a little into the earth. It would only help make the tomatoes grow heavier next season.

But her poor, small monkey is as wan as sand—his fur nearly the same color as the rubbery skin around his little mouth. And he is so very fetal. The rounded, fluffed end of his tail almost touches his brow, as if he had tried to turn in on himself to begin again. The soil beneath him had darkened with his melted ice, and Faye knew that his ice, his water, is meant to sink into the ground of her garden and no one else's. He could easily have fallen twenty feet over in the onion and chive rows of her neighbor who still remains on her porch, on the phone, breaking the privacy of this moment. But he didn't fall into the neighbor's garden. No, he is meant for Faye's garden, his water meant for her soil, and under the earthy surface, the trickles of his water weave around roots and over mole tunnels to meet with the trickles of her own blood. And together the trickles form a stream, his water remembering a distant Heaven, her blood remembering a dead son, and together their stream will drive straight down toward the center of the earth as if it had gushed from the ribs of Christ himself. And no one will ever know this except for Faye and her small, dead monkey.

Her father stood motionless in the doorframe of the kitchen, the most logical place to stand in the event of an earthquake, according to Tim. And the earth still seemed to shake beneath her, even there outside the bathroom, in the kitchen, in front of that baking oven. Her hands still trembled, even though she now held a wooden spoon, and cradled an old mixing bowl to hide her stomach even though she was not foolish enough to believe that she would be showing so soon.

She had planned on baking a German chocolate cake for dessert in hopes that he would both delight in the taste and distract himself by railing against Germany and all the atheists of Europe. Maybe she could find shelter at the center of a storm. A cake was a fragile plan, but it was a plan nonetheless.

Her father watched her, watched her. He said, in almost a whisper, "Don't drop that bowl."

All of Faye's words stuck at the wet base of her lungs. Uttering a single sentence would make her burst again into tears. She couldn't reveal anything, not in front of him, so she balanced her brittle silence like a lump on the back of her tongue.

"Your hands don't look steady. That was my grandmother's bowl. She was a forthright woman. Hard worker. No secrets." Now he actually begun to whisper, his voice creaking like a rocking chair. "Don't drop it, Faye. Don't drop it, Faye. Don't drop it, Faye."

For a moment, she had clarity and calmness enough to allow rational thought into her mind: Just how had he known how to break her? How had he known exactly when?

"Don't drop it, Faye."

Then everything broke.

> And behold a great red dragon, having seven heads and ten horns, and seven crowns upon his heads. And his tail drew the third part of the stars of heaven, and did cast them down to the earth: and the dragon stood before the woman which was ready to deliver, for to devour her child as soon as it was born.
> —Revelations 12:3-4

The doctors and Tim talked about her condition as if she were not lying on the bed in front of them. Tim tussled and twisted the top of his own hair; the doctors kept nodding, then shaking, their heads, the white room lights dancing weirdly off their metal headpieces and shiny framed glasses. They seemed to hover over only one of the choices as if it were an inescapable revelation, and they took turns repeating: We don't have a choice. We have no choice. We don't have a choice.

She called for him. "Tim?"

Tim made shushing sounds. He swooped down to her, scooped her arm in his, and petted her hair away from her eyes. "Quiet now, baby."

"Tim, I know what y'all are talking about." She felt as if she said, "Do not let them," but she knew her words slurred.

"Baby, honey, any other option would require a miracle. A miracle, Faye. There is no other option."

"He's my baby."

"What we're talking about is your life. It's your life we're talking about. And it's not a he, baby. At least no one knows, anyway. I know things are fuzzy to you right now, but trust me. It's your life against impossible odds. We're talking about smack-down out-of-the-clear-blue, falling star, impossible odds, honey. You have to let me do what's best."

"But I believe in miracles."

"You're on morphine."

She sets an unused, round hatbox beside her monkey's little body, and she removes the lid evenly, carefully. Then she lays a hand towel over him and softly shovels her arm under to lift him. She swaddles him tightly then props him in the crook of her elbow.

With her fingertip she pets his hair away from his closed, nutshell eyes. But the hair returns to its own pattern of swirls.

She lowers him onto his side in the hatbox, and grains of dirt fall from her forearm and scatter in dry taps across the bottom of the box.

As she carries her monkey in his hatbox inside the house, Tim stands back and talks rationally at her. She remains silent, and the farther she walks from Tim, the more his questions sprout into sharp warnings, the more, "Shouldn't you reconsider this?" turns into, "Stop. Come here, right now."

Without saying so, she wishes, then, that some shining knight would descend from the clouds too, and that it would slay Tim.

The voice came out of a heaven-white cloud that smelled cold like rubbing alcohol.

"You made it through everything just fine."

"My baby?"

"You made it through just fine, Mrs. Swanson. The procedure went as planned. We're very pleased with the results."

She said, "Dead."

"You made it through just fine."

"He's hitting me in the stomach."

"No one is hitting you. You are under some pain, and you need to rest."

"It was my father. All because he hit me in the stomach. I dropped it and he hit me and hit me in the stomach. Isn't it?"

"No, no. Only natural complications, like we discussed. It wasn't from any trauma, I promise you. It's just a thing that happens randomly. It happens in nature. It's biology."

"Then it's Tim."

There is grandeur in this view of life, with its several powers, having been originally breathed by the Creator into a few forms or into one; and that, whilst this planet has gone cycling on according to the fixed law of gravity, from so simple a beginning endless forms most beautiful and most wonderful have been, and are being evolved.
—Charles Darwin, *The Origin of Species*

What species of monkey is he? It seems rude not to know—un-motherly in fact. She had locked the bedroom door and now kneels beside the bed, elbows propped on the mattress beside her monkey in his hatbox, and she leafs through the pages of Tim's book for the answer. For all the brimstone she had heard about this book growing up, and for all the praise she had heard since Tim, she figures there would have been more to it. Surely it would have exhaustive charts of all possible species. Instead she finds one underlined sentence at its very end, and instead of answering her question, the passage changes it.

What species of monkey am I?

She had been fixed to this planet in accordance with gravity her entire life. She had cycled around the gravity of her father, whose weight bent the air around him, whose soul was so dense that it seemed to pull the very blood out of her. She had cycled around the gravity of Tim, whose brain sent her into orbit through space, leaving her unable to touch any anchored body. And every gravity that moved her had only accumulated. It solidified in layers over her, could have been counted in years like the rings of a tree except the layers that weighed her down were as transparent as ice: blurred, indistinct, cold. And within her frozen block of gravity, she knew she was not his species of monkey. She could never have been any wonderful form of life from the sky.

But there is a grandeur in the way a womb wraps every living creature into the same curve, into a common form.

The Creator's great nostrils had inflated the atmosphere, had filled her stomach with breath not unlike the way her monkey had been filled—filled with enough breath to keep him floating in the air until October 26th, until he was pulled down to the planet by Faye's gravity alone. A primordial, common breath had remained in both of them until they could converge again, here. Now.

The door hammers the room with noise.

"Faye. Open this thing."

The door quakes.

"Faye, I want to think this over with you. We can bury it if you want. I'll even make a little cross for it if I have to, but it is not staying in this house. Faye? Faye! You are being completely irrational. Faye!"

She takes the hatbox with her into the closet, wedges the door shut, and burrows deep into the cave of gowns and raincoats, a place as dark as space. With her entire body, she encircles his round box. She lowers her head near him and breathes the odor of his soil deep into her nostrils. The voice from the bedroom door is now only a distant muffle. The dark is absolute.

Her father stood over her. She could hear the fumes pouring from his mouth.

He said, "It's over now, girl."

He was right. Even though the pain lingered, kept her curled tightly on the kitchen floor, it was over. She would leave his house for all time. She had ridden his violence out until its end.

The rumbles in the distance could be the bedroom door. It could be Tim. It could be that he kicks open the locked bedroom door and that his foot follows the door, and he catches himself, hunched over in still tension like a hungry savage, standing in the doorframe in the middle of his earthquake, an earthquake that could force the upheaval of every piece of ground and turn it all on itself again.

Her father said, "I shouldn't even have to bring the rod to you like this. You shouldn't even have secrets, in the first place, so sinful that you'd take a beating to keep them. Not any daughter of mine. It don't make any sense that you should be under my roof anymore."

The kitchen tile squeaked against her face as she nodded. He made perfect sense.

The closet door opens and the splash of light breaks her eyes. On the closet floor, she curls tighter around her monkey's box and says, "You can't take him. God damn you, Tim, you can't take him."

"Jesus, Faye. Look at you." Tim kneels and crawls closer to her.

She flinches.

"What are you doing? Faye, look at me in the eyes. Look at us. What the hell are we doing?"

"If you hadn't opened that door to let the air in, he would have started to move. He would have touched my nose with his little cold palm. He would have wiggled his fingers."

"What?"

"He was a miracle."

"We need to get you to a hospital. This is not how you are. This is not how we are."

"Maybe, but everything's changed now. Evolution is the end."

"That's not what evolution means, Faye. That doesn't make any sense. Nothing has changed at all except that you have a dead animal in a box. Listen, I want to give you a minute and calm down. I know everything must seem fuzzy to you right now, but I'm not going to drag you out of here or force that monkey out of your hands or anything because you need to show me that you can do this right now. All right? You need to decide how this is going to end."

"It's already ended," she says, as she looks at Tim's primate face, formed from clay by divine hands in the image of the almighty Creator who Himself evolved from apes. In the beginning, all species were one, just like in the end, all men are one, Tim and her father, and just like, by the end, all things are dead that change.

BLACKBEARD IN REPOSE

<u>Retirement, June 1718</u>: Edward Teach, better known as Blackbeard, receives the king's pardon for his career of piracy, having given up his ship, abandoning those loyal to him who were still wild for piracy, and retiring among the quiet plantations of North Carolina.

<u>Two months later, August 1718</u>: A warrant is issued for Blackbeard's arrest on new charges of piracy.

<u>Three months later, November 1718</u>: Blackbeard is killed in what is perhaps the most spectacular pirate battle at sea in history.

She was a planter's daughter, pale as a wave crest, surely no older than sixteen, and upon seeing her whipping white bed sheets over clotheslines alongside the slave women, Blackbeard considered not raping her but, perhaps, marrying her.

He made his way up the hill, the grass under his bootheels feeling more slippery than the fox'ole planks ever did even in a storm, his land legs not yet with him. He neared her. The slave women noticed him first, and they ran off behind the far side of the plantation house, leaving piles of wet sheets still in their baskets, leaving the planter's daughter alone. Blackbeard stood not a whip's length behind her. He said, "Where is your father?"

She started, seeming to come out of some adolescent daydream, turning to see her companions gone and a man squared up to her who was not of this world. He stood as imposing as a locked door, legs cocked apart, cutlass at his hip, chest like a bull's, slinged with a bandoleer heavy with half a dozen flintlocks, his arms shaggy and tensed, and his beard—oh the beard—like a forest soaked in pitch. Matted locks hung among the mass of coarse frays in his beard, with ends charred like cold cigars, bright red and purple ribbons tied around bundles of hair here and there in pigtails. And over the man was a hat, wide like the spread of night. She looked as if she were going to scream, and such an odd sensation in her stomach must have emboldened her. She said, "How do you do, sir? My father is out in the fields."

"Then bring me inside for food and drink, for I am fresh off the sea and am in need of modest but constant quantities of rum and meats. We shall wait for your father there."

"You are fresh off the sea?"

"Smell my beard," he said, "the salt." He fluffed the end of his locks toward her.

Skittishly, she leaned forward and breathed in with her nose. Then she closed her eyes and breathed again. "Fresh off the sea. . ."

"More or less. I have come from the governor's, and it is time now for a wife and a house and some land."

"But what are your intentions here, sir?"

"I intend to have your father give you to me in marriage."

"But do you have a house already? Do you have land already?"

Blackbeard said, "Why? Do I need them?"

"To make your way on the land, sir, you first need land."

He laughed. "Then your father must give me a day to prepare. Tell him I'll be back for you tomorrow at dusk. Tell him to have the sky pilot ready."

"Have what ready, sir?"

"The minister."

And before the lightning bugs had set in that evening, the neighboring family, the Tanners, were leaving their estate in a hastily-packed wagon with a chest full of gold, driving toward Charlotte. When Blackbeard had presented them with the chest, he had said, "Think of this as an exodus. I am Moses come to free you from your servitude to the land. Retire with luxury in the city."

Mr. Tanner had said, "But I was born to the fields. I am a born farmer."

"Anyone can change," Blackbeard said. "Especially in retirement."

"But why is there rust all over the coins?"

"Gold doesn't rust. Blood does."

Mr. Tanner said, "And the idea is to paint no more fresh blood on it? That I should not chance the angel of death when I can simply leave the land of Egypt."

"Are you saying I am not Moses but the angel of death?"

Mr. Tanner said nothing. He looked away, picked up his cane, and poked the end of it into the chest of gold, tapping the bottom and stirring the coins.

"Landlubbers are wiser than I thought," Blackbeard said with a laugh. "And by the by, would you and the lady be so kind as to leave your wedding rings behind?"

There were three great things about rum.

First were the songs.

Second, the pain felt good. The bones in Blackbeard's knees turned warm; the gummy teeth in the back of his jaws turned to iron; the blood he coughed was molten ore. On his gentler nights he would make his men toe the line with him, giving them the first swing, their quick knuckles in his flesh feeling as assuring as spice on his tongue. He enjoyed being slugged more than he enjoyed feeling them crumple under his own fist, and it only ever took one punch from him. Not a single man on his ship could return a second punch, or perhaps they were too afraid to try, and either way it made him more of a man than most alive.

Third, rum made everything feel like skimming the high seas leeward on a running wind. A closed room could be a new shoreline, each conversation an adventure. He climbed over the bow one night, drunker than the sea herself, having just raided a king's cotton vessel, the stores beneath in the *Revenge* now filled with water, flour, salted porks, black powder, a goat, and two Africans. He straddled the figurehead, riding her like a whore, and he howled at the horizon, knowing that no man had ever floated on that point of the earth and had howled like that, had given back such an echo to the bottomless universe. He felt as though there were enough room inside of him to contain an entire Heaven and an entire Hell. Or at least an entire Hell.

There were three terrible things about rum.

First was the bottom.

Second, the crew hid their treacherous wills a little less. Any man-one-of-them would have killed all the others for a chance at command, given the opportunity, and, true, such hunger was needed for a ship of pirates, but it was taxing on the man who held command. Some nights Blackbeard could feel it in the air like an oncoming storm. He could sense that they saw a sign of weakness in him, even if it were naught but a fantasy of theirs, and he could sense their lust for his downfall. At his most melancholic, alone, he had to be stronger than all of them together at their best. One night he ordered the strongest and most violent of the men down into the holds with him, on rocks of the ballasts, and he had the rest bring in pots of brimstone alight. He closed them together with himself in that dark chamber, sulfur fumes taking over the air, their lungs filling with poison, their limbs wracked with convulsions. Outside the rest of the crew waited, murmuring to each other and to their God, wondering who would be first to flee from the chamber, wondering who would be last, hoping it would not be Blackbeard who emerged from that fuming pit victorious after all the rest had fled, but knowing it would be. And while they sat there in the dark, in the stink of such hellish smoke, with their stomachs wrenching, with vomit and bile issuing from their nostrils, with fingers and toes curling back against their wills, there, Blackbeard laughed. And he laughed. The men thought it was the devil himself in there with them, summoned by the alchemy of brimstone and pain, coming to collect on their sins, and at that thought Blackbeard laughed harder and deeper. He thought, *No, men, the devil is not here with us. The devil is at home in his Hell, like a soft, drowsy magistrate. In the Hell that he made, he tortures others. In the Hell that I make, no one suffers greater than I.*

Third, time became apparent. Otherwise, on sober days on the sea, time did not exist. The rising and falling of the sun was nothing more than a bit of reliable weather, no different from the wind and less useful. But when drinking rum, thoughts fell in place as a succession of years, and the bottle itself seemed to whisper: *This taste will run dry, and all your gold will be spent away, and one day you, Blackbeard, will wither and be no more. You have not much longer. Quit this quick sea; spend the years you have left in leisure; stretch them long on upon the land. Find peace for once, and rest yourself there until you fade away like the stars at dawn.*

Blackbeard stood facing all in attendance at the wedding, wearing his same sea-worn outfit, flintlock bandoleers and all, except that he wore a fine velvet coat over it, bright blue, which he had taken off the fresh corpse of an old fat English lord. Blackbeard had not even killed that one; the lord's weak, sickly heart had given out on its own at the sight of him. Blackbeard would never let his own brawny body grow as weak and sick as this lord had let his. But the lord did have good taste in buttons: a year later, on this wedding day that Blackbeard could never have predicted for himself, they were still shiny.

All the landlubbers in their seats were silent. The minister behind him was silent. His bride and her father were soon to come out of the house's doors and down the aisle in the yard to him, but the waiting was disastrous on Blackbeard's ears. The crickets never stopped ratcheting, the cicadas never stopped hissing, the bullfrogs never stopped drumming, and the people never stopped saying nothing.

"Has anyone started on the rum yet?" Blackbeard asked.

A few heads shook *no*. No one spoke.

"It's from the finest stores in the West Indies. We shall get to it soon. Just have patience."

They said nothing.

Blackbeard checked his lard-slicked hair, and he slicked it back again for good measure. These people would never be friends with him.

Out of the doors came the young girl in her wedding dress, arm in arm with her father, who looked long sick with something. Blackbeard had seen that type of sickness before in his own mother, the kind that allowed one to slowly plan for death. This farmer's skeletal face looked little different than his mother's had in her last autumn. Blackbeard himself felt as robust and fit as he had ever been, but when he locked eyes with the father, he knew his own body now counted for little. Blackbeard and this father felt the same thing and knew it. Somehow, their souls were in the same antechamber, their hearts already accepting the same, impending end.

The girl looked excited, or, perhaps, simply not bored for the first time in her life, but her father's face was as solemn as everyone else's. The ceremony went quickly, as Blackbeard had ordered, and even though the young girl's smell filled his nose, a smell of honeysuckle, he could only concentrate his mind on the sea of silent, stern faces behind him. They were faces that seemed incapable of hearty laughter, incapable of lusty jeers, incapable of keeping him company in the coming years.

The minister had finished and told Blackbeard that he may kiss his bride. Blackbeard looked on all the marble-like faces in attendance, and he had an immediate desire to give up on them and snort like a wild boar, so he gave up on them and snorted like a wild boar. He grabbed the girl, his wife, by her waist, lifted her in the air, and smashed her lips to his ravenously. Then he hoisted her over his shoulder like a bag of spoils and gave a thunderous, throaty roar right in the faces of the audience. His flying spittle

landed on the shoes and pants of some plantation owners
and on their wives in the front row.

The girl on his shoulder kicked her legs and laughed
and squealed. He strode to the barrel of rum, kicked off
the lid, and scooped a whole bowl of it to his face. He
scooped up a second bowl and flung it at the people in
attendance, sprinkling them as if it were an anointing.
"Come," he yelled. "Who among you has so much life left
as to enjoy wasting it with idleness?"

No one answered.

Blackbeard locked eyes with the bride's slowly dying
father, saying, "For a man hath no better thing under the
sun than to eat, and to drink, and to be merry."

And as if those words of Ecclesiastes were a direct order
from a captain of theirs, the bride's father went for the
rum, and then the rest of the people came, even hurried, to
the feast laid out before them on the long oak tables. There
sat ready and steaming bowls of potatoes, plates of charred
fowl, fillets of smoked fish, buckets of boiled crab, slabs of
ribs and bacon; there were bowls of cherries and apples
and peaches. Growlers of beer scattered the place-settings,
and the oak barrels of rum sat close enough for many to
reach without walking far. The people seemed to follow
Blackbeard's rhythm: he poured rum down his bride's
throat, and they spurred each other to drink; he shoveled
up handfuls of sliced apples, and they ate with their bare
hands; he tore at his bride's dress, and they tore at the skin
of the full roast pig. Others began howling with causeless
laughter as he and his bride did.

As the moon emerged that evening, Blackbeard pulled
a flintlock from his bandoleer and fired it into the sky,
pausing the party.

They all watched him.

Then he tossed another loaded flintlock to some nearby
landlubber, a toothless old lady in a cotton bonnet, and he
gestured toward the moon. The lady pulled back the pistol's
hammer and fired at the sky. Everyone roared with delight,
and they took back to drinking and shoving and eating

and even fighting all the more shamelessly. Blackbeard smiled. There was a little bit of pirate in everyone.

It was the fourth party of the week, and everyone within earshot of Blackbeard's cannon was there. They danced in his dining room. They danced in the halls. They sang on the front porch and meandered in couples on the lawn. The slaves continually filled goblets and furnished trays of food. On some of these nights, Blackbeard would dominate the festivities, but on nights like this one, he simply ambled about, enjoying the noise and the chaos.

As with most nights, his young wife went about the party on her own as a queen among people who were until recently her betters. They would laugh when she laughed, and they would cause foolish mischief when she tossed a gold coin at them to do so.

In the largest room of the house, which was once a sitting room but which had been stripped bare to make a ballroom, a finely groomed man in a purple coat and tasseled boots stopped Blackbeard as he walked alone and begged for him to come nearer. He said, "They tell me you had made a living on the sea. A blessedly successful merchant, I presume."

Blackbeard studied the man carefully, trying to remember if he had met him before. He said, "Not precisely."

"Well good riddance to it nonetheless, don't you say? I can tell by the look of you that the sea does not suit you. You look firmly planted on the ground." He said it as a compliment, as a toast for cheers, for he raised his blackjack mug to tap against Blackbeard's. But he lifted his mug alone.

"Is that what you see when you look at me? A man made for the solid earth?"

"Yes. And none better, I say!" He shook his mug in the air again. "In fact, and I say this with all sincerity, you are made for politics, my man. Have you thought about taking up a magistrate position? You would be governor in a year's time." He turned to the folks behind him and yelled, "How many among us think our gracious host here, Master

Edward Teach, would make the finest politician North Carolina has ever seen?"

The crowd raised their hands and their drinks and their voices in agreement.

Then he said, "The votes are in! Three cheers for our future governor! Hip-hip. . ."

And the crowd cheered in orderly fashion.

After they had finished their third cheer, when they were waiting for his response to them, Blackbeard gave an exaggerated, courtly bow. The audience seemed delighted at this, clapping and then turning to each other for continued socializing. The party carried on. Blackbeard went down into the cellar of the house and vomited in a barrel of pickles. He stayed down there in the hull of the house, alone, for the rest of the night.

Back on the *Queen Anne's Revenge*, there was a night that Blackbeard had dined in his quarters with the best man of the crew, Israel Hands, and the most dastardly man of his crew, Pinckney Anak. It was at the end of a fine day. They had taken a Spanish trading ship only three days before, and earlier that morning they had been burying a chest of gold in a dry, sandy cave on some unnamed island. Blackbeard had never before done that—buried treasure— and he would never do it again, but he wanted to do it and draw the map to it himself just the once so that he might answer yes if ever asked about such a thing. When they had finished with burying the gold, they had found a waterfall, had bathed in those heavy, pelting waters, and had proceeded to light the surrounding fern-thickets and woodlands on fire. The walls of flame spread so quickly that Blackbeard and his men were forced to run to the shore, to run truly for their lives. From the ship, the burning island looked like a glowing-hot city of brass.

So there in his quarters at dinner, his men laughed and feasted and boasted. They acted like men who had the world by the throat, men who would dare to call themselves immortal, and Blackbeard as well felt full of strange lighting. The meal was simple but superb in its honesty: bananas, wild boar from the island that morning, Spanish rum from the taken ship, a still-steaming loaf of bread as large as a baby and as wonderfully sour-tasting as the bread his own mother used to bake. They smoked from their own hand-carved pipes to finish. The candlelight winked at Blackbeard, egging him on to do something worthy to finish the day, something to punctuate the feeling. As they pushed away their empty plates, Blackbeard leaned forward and blew out the candles. The room went black. He pulled two pistols under the table, cocked them, and fired into the dark. Pinckney Anak had been wily enough to flee the room the moment Blackbeard had blown out the candles, but Israel Hands took a lead ball to the knee. He never walked right again.

Weeks later, Israel had asked Blackbeard why he had done such a thing, whether it had been nothing more than depraved sport. Blackbeard had answered that, true, it had been a bit of sport, but it was also something more: it was needed, lest they fail to realize the difference in their coming days and years between just living and really living, where the edge of death is a great and fine thing.

Israel said, "Then it was in truth needless, captain. I know well both my own mortality and the difference between a full life and an empty life. I need no reminding."

"But one day," Blackbeard said, "I might."

In North Carolina, in the once-fine plantation house that had begun falling apart around him in only a few weeks' time, while his wife was he knew not where, Blackbeard dined with twelve of the richest men along the coast, one of them an inventor of agricultural implements, two others members of European royalty. One of the older men, a slave-dealer, had brought along a catamite to play the fiddle while they ate. The mood was solemn and the meal extravagant: beer-boiled crab, corn pies, mutton piled into hollowed-out watermelons, an aged hock of a black-hooved Iberian hog from the acorn fields of Portugal, a wine bottled by the man who killed the last dodo, and Cuban cigars to finish. The men around the table talked of the food and drinks and cigars as if those things were adventures, as if consuming them were some meaningful travel or risk, as if this meal would stay in their memory, but Blackbeard had forgotten already what the appetizer was before he had even stood up from his chair, and all he could think about were dinners in his quarters on the *Queen Anne's Revenge*.

While these men talked, Blackbeard leaned over the table and blew out the candles. The room went black. He pulled two pistols under the table, cocked them, and he thought. About what, it was not clear; it was a cloudy thought, as rough an outline as the drawing of the dodo bird on the wine bottle.

The men at the table had gone silent. The catamite continued to play in the dark. Perhaps he was blind.

Blackbeard rubbed his callused finger-pads lightly on the triggers, but then he flicked open the flash-pans and let the powder spill from his pistols. Within moments, the men were laughing. They began to thank Blackbeard for being such a lively, adventurous fellow, a dinner with him better than a night at the theater. They continued to eat and talk in the dark, but Blackbeard had already walked from the room quietly.

He went down to the river and sat on the soggy ground among the cattails, only momentarily disturbing the sounds around him, the frogs soon bellowing again and the crickets soon ratcheting again, as if this lowly place did not understand that the black king of the sea, more feared than Death himself, deigned to sit there. He pulled a third pistol, a loaded one, and put the muzzle in his mouth. He cocked it. And then he noticed a great but silent movement in the dark of the river, perhaps a flatboat of some sort. He parted the reeds and saw that it was in fact a flatboat, and it looked to be carrying a load of tobacco and a crew of no more than three, maybe four, men. No doubt that this boat, and others like it, would be returning the other way with full crop payments aboard in flimsy chests. To hijack such boats and make off with all the spoils, on a river like this against a river-crew like that, well, such a plunder would take at least a light raft, powder, bags, and four or five armed, vicious young men. Either it would take all that, or just one good pirate.

He had nearly finished knotting the bright new bows around the locks in his beard when his young wife came in the room. She lifted a porcelain vase from the bedstand and threw it at his feet. The thing shattered, the old water from it soaking his boots and making his heels feel oddly familiar.

She said, "Those are my ribbons."

"Not when they're in my beard."

"Where are you going, dressed like that? Where have you been these last nights?"

"I've been away from here," he said. "And I'm going to go farther away."

"And me? What of me?"

Blackbeard looked at her through the mirror. Her eyes looked years older now, despite its having been no more than seven weeks since their marriage. She might have all the makings of a vicious character, a scoundrel, a razor-boned beauty who could take from the world as she pleased. Then again, she may just be another simple soul meant only to be forgotten, as Blackbeard had nearly forgotten her already. The choice would have to be hers. He said, "I think I might have actually loved you when I first saw you, on the lawn, whipping out those white sheets like sails. And I know now that when I love something once, I love it always."

"I think that you, my love, are the devil. I knew that when I first saw you."

"Good." He went to her and lifted her over his shoulder as he had on their wedding day.

She hammered her fists against his back and kicked her legs and called him a bastard son of a whore and laughed. He laughed. He walked her out of the room and paused at the edge of the staircase, waiting for her to gather a sense of their height, and then he bounded wildly down the stairs with her, skipping two steps at a time, sending her into a squealing frenzy on his shoulder, making them both feel like they were falling off the end of a plank. When they landed, she was breathless and still trying to laugh.

He carried her farther on to the basement, down those steps a little more carefully, and there in the mildewed air and the false dusk-light, she stopped laughing and cursing. He set her down onto her own two feet. He noticed they were bare. They were long feet, actually. She may have more to grow yet.

"What are you doing with me? You're going to lock me down here, aren't you? Never to see me again?"

Blackbeard said, "Most true."

"So be it," she said. "There's food enough down here for days. I'll make so much noise that even your drunkest guests will come looking for me."

"That's good, my love, but you'll have to do better than that." He dug through his coat pockets. "As for me, I've been haunted as of late by too many thoughts. Reflections. I did not have them until I came here, until I first saw you, so I shall leave them with you, if it's possible to give away such things. If not, then at least make use of this." He produced a folded paper and let it fall on the steps. "May your life be a storm and your death be a grand one."

She watched him leaving slowly back up the basement steps, up toward that door he was surely going to lock. She said, "Where will you go?" But he did not answer. Instead, he left as he said he would, though she was unsure what to expect of his leaving those reflections that haunted him. He shut the door behind him, worked the lock, and dropped something with a light clinking noise just outside the door.

She listened carefully a bit longer, and she heard him crashing and clanking things about up there, perhaps overturning furniture, perhaps knocking over lamps and candelabras. Even though she tried, she never heard the final moment in which he left the house for good, in which he left, certainly, to return to the waters, where she imagined the houses moved with the wind and were pulled along by the constellations, where he had been the black king of the sea, a crown of bones on his brow, a necklace of thorns clamped on his throat, the shadow of his flag like the fall of a storm on the unwary ships of the world. May his future be like his past that he missed so dreadfully.

As for her own future, she would have to reflect in more immediate terms. She could already smell the fire that he had set tearing through the house above her. She climbed the steps enough to get eye-level with the gap at the foot of the locked door, and the orange light glinted off of what must be a key that he had dropped out there, but the black smoke began to obscure her view already, seeping through the cracks in the panels. She surveyed the basement quickly for anything that might be of use: a rope, a flimsy broom, useless barrels and jars and buckets, the folded paper he had left on the steps—she picked it up. It was a hand-drawn map, a map that could be slid under the door, perhaps to get at that key. If she were going to make it out alive, and after that, if she were going to make it in such a world on her own, maybe even to get revenge, then she would have to be as cunning and as fearless as Blackbeard—she would have to make of herself a pirate.

NEW DAYS OF THE WOLF

Roman doesn't feel entirely together as he swoops through the house, gathering stacks of reports, tugging his already looped tie over his head, balancing a frozen bagel on the rim of his coffee mug to catch the steam, wishing, between mental to-do lists, that he were required to pack a pistol—or some artifact of authority—to work, and thinking that he should in fact study to become a detective or a cop with all the extra time he now has since his wife finally moved out and took their daughter with her, and he rushes through the utility room and clamps hold of his sport coat with his shoulder and chin, and he thumbs through his key ring for the only car key she left him with, which goes to the only car still in his garage, her unimpressive ten-year-old sedan, and he steps down into his garage, and there it is, moving inside the car—a blur, gray, thrashing in the front seats. It's a wolf.

He drops his sport coat and loses the pile of reports to the concrete floor, but he still balances his coffee and bagel. The wolf lunges within the car; Roman flinches, palms out, at the sight of the wolf, as if to keep it from eating him.

But he is still in one piece, so he lowers his hand to see the wolf in the driver's seat barking in violent cracks. It twists its head and snaps its bared teeth. Its neck and back bristle. Roman doesn't see the wolf's eyes at all—only its stark front teeth.

He bends at the knees, lowering his gravity to slow things down. He sets his mug and bagel lightly on the concrete and scoots it an inch toward the wolf, and he feels a passing pride from not having dropped his breakfast in panic. He can see, now, that the insides of the windows and windshield are all covered in desperate streaks of dried blood. He gets a glimpse of the seats that have exploded in the car, at the countless chunks of foam, spotted with blood, that fill the car like snow. The wolf has been trying to escape all night.

He leans for a closer view. The wolf jerks at him again and tries to chew him apart through the glass, but its teeth merely smack against the flat pane. He stumbles back, sees the impression of ribs through the wolf's hide. Actually, its entire skeleton seems evident somehow, nearly bones for legs. It must be starving.

He retreats through the utility room, into the kitchen, hurries to the phone. Dials. Waits. Between rings the receiver echoes the sound of his sprinting breaths, making him aware for the first time that he is in fact breathing, that his heart is drumming.

The voice that picks up on the other end is as dead as marble. "Charlotte Chamber of Commerce. How may I help you?"

"I won't be in today. Roman. I got to go."

"Roman? You know what day this is. The roundtable, the trustees, the Wells Fargo deal. That's your baby. You can't not come in."

He can't just let the wolf starve in there. He has to feed it.

"No one's life is on the line," he says. "Just tell Morgan for me."

"Uh, your ass is on the line," the voice says. "There is no way I'm telling him you're leaving us hanging. You tell him. I'm transferring you now."

Roman eyes the fridge, x-raying its contents, recalling this week's meals. He did have that Hamburger Helper night. Were there any leftovers? He reaches for the fridge door and pulls the phone with him, and the cord springs and coils, frustrating his arms. He rips and yanks and finally disconnects the damn thing. On the bottom shelf beside a six-pack of protein shakes and a half-empty vodka bottle, there is a tupperware bowl; there are leftovers.

In the garage, in the car, the wolf stands poised and growling. Its lips roll even farther along its gums, exposing that trap of teeth. Roman circles the car with soft steps, and he extends the bowl of Hamburger Helper in front of him like a medicine man's offering. He orbits as far from the wolf as possible, to the passenger's side back door, and although the wolf aims its muzzle and follows Roman's movements, it remains on the driver's seat.

"Good. Just stay where you are," he tells the wolf. He needs to open the car door only slightly, just a crack, in order to pour the leftovers into the back seat. It should be enough to hold the wolf over until he can find some real food for it. What do wolves even eat in the wild? Rabbits? No, not what do they eat, but how much? The wolf's body is pulling so viciously at every moment that it can't have a single spare calorie beyond the flesh of its own stomach, and surely a night thrashing in this car has pushed the poor thing against the window of death.

He notices the orange stickers above the interior door handles are exposed, that the car is unlocked, and he feels a cold mix of relief and worry that the wolf has not pawed the handle and let itself out, not yet.

Roman lifts the door handle silently. "It's okay," he says. "Food, see? Just stay where you are."

The wolf snarls, its ribcage expanding and contracting, pumping faster. Roman's nervous breathing matches the wolf's. He eases the door and breaks the seal of air. An odor of musk escapes the slight opening. He risks the car door open just a little bit more and tips the bowl over the top of it, slopping the Hamburger Helper clump by clump onto the edge of the seat, the floorboard, and down to the garage floor.

And the wolf is on him that fast. It smashes against the inside of the door, biting, barking, practically running in place against him. Roman shoves his entire body against the door, trying to hold back the storm of limbs and noise. His feet slip over concrete, slip fast over noodles and meat, and he too feels as though he is running in place. Only the thin window separates their equally pressed faces, their nearly touching wild eyes, as each now beholds the other.

In a quick latch, the door shuts. The wolf is enclosed inside the car again, safely separated from Roman. Falling on the garage floor, he dry heaves, spits out only empty bile, and lies flat on the concrete to recover his breath, to relax his muscles, as the wolf's muffled barks dwindle, dwindle, a brief sleep of shock.

The grocery store seems much busier for a weekday than he would have imagined, and Roman, hoping that the taxi out front does wait for him, relies on the flash of an extra twenty and a nod to the driver as contract enough.

He carts to the butcher's counter and disregards the tiny service bell. "Marty." He tries to stretch his voice into the back room without yelling, hoping to avoid the attention of anyone else. "Hey, Marty, you in today?"

Marty waddles through the stainless swing-doors and rubs his palms together, warming them. "Roman, the five card stud! I've been waiting forever on that next goddamn poker game already. Wow, are you all right, man?"

"Hey, I got a weird order for you." Roman leans over the counter and drops his voice. "Favor, actually. I need a lot of wild meat. Forget the cost. I don't care. Wild meat like rabbits and caribou. You know?"

"Caribou?"

"There's something happening with me that I can't even talk about." Roman cuts a look at the ladies browsing the nearby aisles. He feels undercover; his tone gains authority. "You just got to trust me. Get me a lot of meat with skin and all, no questions asked."

Marty shows his hands, empty. "All right, man. Okay, I know I can get at least one rabbit from my brother's place, and I got plenty of lamb. You think you can settle for beef steaks instead of caribou? I do have some ground buffalo, but it's frozen."

Roman says, "All right, listen. Here's the deal, just between us: there's a wolf in my wife's car."

"She okay?"

"No, it's in my car. She left me. I took a taxi."

"*Left you* left you?"

"She was sleeping with her lawyer. Long story. Well, not really. I don't know, but it suits me just fine—long time coming. Actually, I'm finally free, you know?"

Marty says, "I would fucking kill both of them, man. Did you at least lay into them, baseball bat or something?"

"No."

"I would've cleavered the guy up, man. Lawyer steaks." Marty's eyes seem to glaze at a scene of coming at invisible people with invisible weapons, and he hacks the air. "Whack, mother fucker. Whack, whack."

Roman watches the scene, unsure. "Yeah."

"But you didn't do *nothing*?"

"No. I said I'm glad she's gone."

"Doesn't fucking matter. You know? A real man, a real man's fucking territory. . ." Marty pauses, flinches.

Roman stands back, his voice low, saying, "I know."

"Ah, shit, man. I'm sorry. I didn't mean that. You're right to let it go. I'm crazy. What about this dog in the car?"

"Wolf. A real wolf. It's wild."

"Shit, what'd the cops say?"

"What would the cops do? I should have been a cop anyway. I think I can handle one goddamn situation in my own goddamn life, Marty. One goddamn situation."

"Yeah, you're right. You're right, man. What would cops do? Hell, I'll have my brother deliver the meat to your place later today. Okay?"

"Thanks a lot, Marty." Roman nods and moves away from the counter, leaving his cart.

"You know what you need, Roman? A good old man-party bachelor night to get over that woman, or whatever. What do you say we get that poker game going this Friday?"

"Can't. I got a wolf to feed."

The fridge is stacked full of raw steaks, slabs of ribs, cellophane-wrapped trout, a whole leg of lamb, even that one dead rabbit, still wearing its fur. The wolf hadn't so much as sniffed at the leftovers Roman had poured into the car, but it will surely devour this tower of meat.

The workbench in his garage is no longer orderly and sterile, no longer a museum to potential manhood. It is now scattered with sawdust and nails, covered with steel tools and planks of wood. It is a mess, and Roman, too, is disheveled in the midst of it, hammering one last, extra nail into his third attempt at a wooden brace, a brace that just has to work this time.

In all the time Roman has spent in the garage since this began, the wolf still has not warmed to him. The most ease it has shown has been its claiming of the back seat, using it to curl for quickly disturbed naps, and to pace.

It paces now, as Roman surveys the space between the car door and the garage wall. Perhaps the reason he hasn't yet been able to construct a functional brace, one to restrain the door from opening wide enough for escape, is that he becomes mesmerized every time he studies the car, mesmerized by the wolf as it paces, yes, as it paces now. It goes back and forth in the back seat, walking only a step or two to one door, then lifting its front quarters and swaying itself in the opposite direction, to the other door, then lifting and turning again. The wolf revolves in that confined space, turning and turning, engenders its own cosmos there, in that same back seat where Roman had once let his wife roll off his condom with her perfect teeth, in the same back seat where she had then turned away and ridden into him at some impossible distance until she was satisfied that it was done, that she had got that daughter out of him.

The wolf revolves.

Between the garage wall and the car door, Roman wedges the brace, a brace that amounts to little more than a wooden rail with legs of its own and reinforced bumpers on either end.

The wolf freezes, baring its teeth. Its throat rumbles, rattles even, like bones in a bag. Roman has been telling it to hold on, hold on, but there's no way the thin beast will make it one more day without food.

Roman tests the brace, finds it sturdy enough, and retrieves a steak from the refrigerator. He tears away the white butcher paper with birthday eagerness. The steak slumps heavily in his hand, bloody and bright. He readies his free hand at the car door handle, and he tries to read the wolf's eyes—those precise, yellow marbles—tries to find eagerness in them, but instead he is drawn back into those teeth.

"I got it this time," he tells the wolf. "Trust me. Stay with me."

He pulls the car door open, and it quickly stops against the brace. The wolf attacks, all claws and jaws, pushing at the door and writhing its body at the narrow gap, but the car door doesn't give. The brace works, and Roman knows it's a job well done, a situation under control. Dispatch, call for back-up to back-off—it took only one man.

He squeezes a steak into the car, poking it through with his index finger and trying to avoid those snapping teeth. The steak breaches the gap and flops onto the wolf's head. The wolf hops back.

Roman shuts the door.

He feels safe enough for the first time to stand against the car, getting to watch the wolf finally eat. He gets to watch the wolf rip into that meat as it seems to want to rip into him. He's sure he will even see the wolf begin to thicken, to pad its sharp bones and fill out the sags in its hide. But Roman sees none of this.

The wolf edges toward the meat, sniffs it, then steps a paw onto it with complete disregard, as if it were

indistinguishable from its snowy floor of foam. The wolf
begins, again, to bark incessantly, full only of hunger and
hate. It barks at him.

The fridge door stands wide open, its racks and shelves
stained the rusty moss of blood, and Roman sits on the tile
in front of it, letting the cold stench of meat waft over him.
The only selections left to stare at now are the leg of lamb
and a lone trout, the rest of the meat having been squeezed
into the car, piece by piece, over the course of two days,
only for the wolf to shun all of its food completely. It has
even ignored the full rabbit that Roman had dangled by
the ears, having hoped to spur the wolf's predatory instincts.
The only aggression it has shown has been toward Roman
himself, who remains unattainable on the safe side of the
car's glass.

  If only he could order it like a K-9 Unit. Stay, he would
say, and it would freeze. Eat, he would say, and it would
dive into the meat and save itself from needless starvation.
But this thing is wild. And he sits so deep in worry that the
knock on the front door doesn't even occur to Roman as
something to acknowledge. Except for acquiring meat, he
hasn't thought of the front door or the world beyond it for
what feels like decades.

  Knocks come from the door, again, more aggressive.

  He slams the fridge shut and hurries to the front door
in order to rid himself of whatever this distraction might
be. He opens the door, and his wife stands on the porch
with their daughter at her side.

  "Let me through, Roman," his wife says. "I need to use
the bathroom bad."

  She pushes her way inside the house and guides her
daughter to Roman, who stands silent, still trying to wake
himself to what is happening. On her way down the hall
she yells, "Forget to pay your phone bill? Jesus, Roman,
look at this place."

  The daughter avoids Roman's eyes. She seems to
entertain herself by fiddling with her tiny pink backpack

that is covered in Japanese symbols and bunny caricatures. She wrinkles her nose at the room around her and says, "Stinks."

Roman, still watching the daughter, yells at his wife in the bathroom, "You come over here just to take a piss or something?"

She yells back at him through the closed door. "It's Friday, Roman. Remember the 'every other weekend' part? That would be today."

He doesn't have time to spend with this daughter, not a whole weekend babysitting. It's out of the question. What he needs to do is to figure out a way to get that wolf to eat something, and he is running out of options. He has offered it every type of dead meat he could find.

"Roman," he hears, "do you even want her here this weekend?"

He reaches down to hold the girl's little hand, and she wriggles away from him. Instinctively he reaches again, faster, and she struggles away. He grabs her arm tight.

"Ouch. Stop it."

Her flesh feels so tender in his grip. And he lets his fingers dig naturally, like teeth, into her arm.

She squeals and struggles harder. Roman forces his hand open to let her loose, and she falls to the floor. Now her face is loud, wailing, full of snotty tears, and she crawls away from him like a wounded rabbit.

"I want her here," Roman says, but the girl's crying is too loud, so he yells over her. "I want her here!"

The wolf barks from the garage, as if it's thinking what he is, and he can't keep his face from filling with delight. He's sharing this moment with his wolf.

His wife charges out of the bathroom. "What the hell are you doing?" She reaches her daughter and kneels, hugging her. "What the fuck did you do to her?" She expects a response but gets none. "Roman. Roman!"

Her tone demands that he look her in the eyes, but Roman continues to stare at her daughter's soft arms, at her nearly pink legs.

"What the fuck is wrong with you? What the hell is that barking? Look at me. Are you drunk?"

Roman says, "She'll be all right. I'll take her this weekend. Leave her."

His wife stands and tugs her daughter up to her hip. "The fuck you will. Come on, sweetie. Daddy's drunk. I'm sorry, sweetie."

Roman braces himself between them and the door, spreading his arms out like lumber in his wife's path. "I said leave her." And now he speaks with authority. "You're *both* staying this weekend."

She mocks a laugh. "You didn't seem to care when we left before."

"I didn't. But I still should have done something. I should have kept you here."

"How? Like winning me back? You're so romantic."

"Like beating the fuck out of both of you. You and your goldmine with a dick, both curled up, begging for the cops. Begging me to stop beating you."

"Jesus, listen to yourself. You need to seriously pull your shit together, Roman. What we are going to do right now is we are going to walk out this door and we are going back home and we are going to—"

"You are home."

"Back to Tim's. And he is going to get on the horn, and by Monday morning he's going to have your visitations ripped out from under your ass until you pull your shit together. Goodbye, Roman. Jesus, look at yourself."

She lugs her daughter and ducks past him, out the door. Roman slams it shut behind her. He breathes heavily through his nostrils. He snarls, breathes. The air is fast, growing faster.

He yanks the door open, and somehow the opening of the door does what he wants: it turns him wild. He runs outside—daylight strikes his eyes. He blinks and shakes it away and charges for her car in the driveway. She shuts her driver's door, her eyes widen at the sight of him, and she slams her hand repeatedly down onto the door lock.

Roman lunges at the car, jerks on the door handle. The engine starts, and the car rolls. He scratches at the windshield, catches the metal wiper—rips back a fingernail and streaks blood across the glass. He can't get to them. The car squeals in reverse down the driveway, away from him, and on the road it jolts forward, peeling away, ticking its wipers to wash away his blood.

Deep after sunset, Roman lies on his couch, petting the gauze that is wrapped around his index finger, and he makes plans on sleeping, on dreaming. He wants to dream of the wolf. He wants to dream that it all happens while he is camping, or at least sitting beside a campfire. He's sitting on a log, in a small clearing, in the middle of an endless woods in the middle of an endless darkness. The only true light in all of space is that one campfire.

In the tree line, a pair of small reflections blink.

"Who goes there?" he demands, smiling, knowing there will be no answer.

Through the curtain of night, a lupine muzzle pushes its way into the flickering orange view. Its eyes shine metallic black, not yellow like they should really be, but utter black. Its ashen fur lifts and falls in waves with each creeping, sinewy step. It is horridly skinny.

"Jesus, look at yourself," he says at the wolf. "You're starving. Don't worry. I have a rabbit in my hat." Roman stands and reaches up to the top hat that is suddenly on his head. He bends at the waist like a great showman and lets the top-hat roll down his arm, catching the brim by the tips of his fingers.

He strides to the wolf and lifts the hat above its head to prepare the wolf for the treat soon to fall from, or even hop out of, the depths of the hat.

The wolf sniffs and lifts its front paws off the ground.

Roman tilts the hat to spill out the rabbit, but nothing happens. He pats the top, shakes it, but nothing comes out.

The wolf leans back further and fully stands on its hind legs. Its arms dangle crookedly at its stomach. Then it levels its head forward with ears sharpened, spreads its jaws, and laughs.

Its cackle is a chorus of sharp sounds.

Roman stumbles backward, terrified, wanting to cover his ears but not doing so. He desperately reaches into his top hat, patting the bare lining and saying, "Stop laughing. Stop it. I have food for you. I can feed you. Just stop that laughing!"

The wolf walks toward him on its hind legs in a gangly fashion. It tilts its head at Roman and speaks, "Oh, yes yes yes." Its voice leaps sporadically like a stretched yelp. "We haves the knowing of polite meats. Hide a riddle of you?"

"What?" Roman says. "I didn't hide any riddle."

"Yours hide, thems hide, alls does us have a hide."

Roman points his finger at the wolf. "What you're going to do is you are going to walk back into those woods and you're going to go back home—"

"But we stand is this home."

"The fuck this is your home," Roman says. "This campfire is mine. Stop talking crazy."

"But we can't talking. We is just the beast." The wolf laughs again, its tongue wagging from its mouth.

"Stop laughing," Roman says.

The wolf weaves its head toward Roman, and walks toward him, toward the fire. Only now does Roman see that his fingernail is missing, and blood pours down from the wound like a faucet. He gasps.

"Now is you hide the riddle?" the wolf says at him.

Roman spreads his arms and braces himself between the nearing wolf and the fire. "Stay away from my campfire." His finger continues to soak the ground with steady blood.

The wolf ducks past Roman, giggling as it gets its head trickled on by the stream of blood. Then it paws its feet in a circle around the campfire, orbiting it.

Roman backs away from its path.

The wolf moves faster, laughing. "Now is you hide the riddle?" It begins a rhythm of bending forward, then tossing its head back. Its speech turns into song, "Now is you hide the riddle, riddle? Now is you hide the riddle?"

"Stop it," Roman yells.

The wolf moves so fast that it now jumps along on its hind legs as it lurches and tosses back and lurches again. "Now is you hide the riddle, riddle?" It leaps and sings, its brush tail fanning the flames, its teeth meeting with hollow clacks. "Now is you hide the riddle?" Its hind legs kick up dust with each joyous bound as it circles the fire to no end.

"Yes," Roman finally cries. "My hide is the riddle!"

And the worst part about the entire night is that Roman tosses and turns on the couch and has no dreams at all.

The garage stinks of rot, stinks of rancid meat. Roman knows that it should make him wretch, but he sniffs deeply and enjoys his guilt. The wolf is poised in the back seat, and although it growls and sporadically barks, it sounds weaker, its aggression more faded than ever. Roman is losing the wolf, and there is nothing he can do about it.

He meanders to the hood of the sedan and steps one foot on top of it. The skin of his bare foot gets purchase on the sleek metal, so he hops completely onto the hood. It gives slightly under his weight as he moves to the windshield and drapes himself belly-down over the roof of the car. He stares through the back window at the upside-down wolf in its upside-down world of blood-streaked glass, and bloody foam snow, and untouched, brown and green meat.

The wolf barks up at Roman's face, but with no more strength than a hiccup. Roman wipes his hand along the window, as if petting the wolf. "I'm sorry," he tells it. "I just don't know."

The poor thing rakes its blood-caked paw at his hand, or maybe the wolf is raking at the white gauze.

"Want this?" Roman unwinds the wrapping from his index finger, and with each turn the wolf perks up more and more. He peels down to the sticky red layers and frees his finger, and the wolf is electrified, biting, barking, yow-yoweling.

Roman waves the string of gauze like a toy and expects the wolf to chase it from within the car, but the wolf stays planted, with front legs propped up between the speakers on the back dash, with hind legs on the seat, standing.

The wolf is biting at Roman's wounded index finger.

"My hide is the riddle," he says.

Roman slides off the car, and at his workbench he tosses the boards and wood-saws and jars of nails out of the way and finds his never-used machete. He wastes no time, lays his index finger flat along a 2x4 board, raises the machete, and takes a solid whack. He wedges the blade out of the wood and picks up the finger before the pain finally wracks his body, shakes his knees and his neck, turns his stomach. The pain makes him hold his breath, makes him spit the air out between his teeth in short spurts.

For the first time since it came to him, the wolf howls. It sits in the back seat and points its head up at its exact meridian in space, its whole body angling toward the tip of its muzzle, God's perfect pyramid. And it fills the world with its deep cry, hollow, as if it rattles the bones of some old world and carves one more tunnel through the sky and into that perfect, silver moon.

Roman pops open the car door, tosses his severed finger through its gap, and slams the door shut. The wolf swoops the finger into its mouth and swallows it whole.

The wolf is finally eating. It will live.

Roman again cracks open the door, secured against the brace he made, and he lets the blood from his fingerless stub trickle into the car. The wolf shoots to him and laps the blood up, sloppy and eager. Roman is nursing the wolf, and he is filled with a flourishing pride that he has never before imagined. He is filled with glory.

He looks toward the machete again and considers his body as if it were a diagram. He imagines dotted lines tracing the correct cuts. Could he spare some toes? A hand even? But he knows the thoughts are ultimately failures.

Even if he could follow through with more, those parts would sustain the wolf for only a short while, and he might bleed to death, leaving it trapped in the car, alone.

But he knows he can do something.

He goes to the garage door and smacks the switch. The chain above him whines, and the door lifts like a curtain. Roman squints in anticipation of the bright noon that the clinking door is slow to reveal, but, surprised, he sees that the world is black, that, yes, it is filled with twinkling stars on lampposts and the sizzle of crickets, but mostly it is empty, a limitless field.

He returns to the wolf, and as it nearly hops up and down, Roman feels his eyes filling with water, feels his throat tighten. He hopes the night, for the wolf, will last long enough, hopes the dark world will be wide enough. And he hopes that, to the wolf, he will taste fresh and new. He hopes that his own meat will fuel the wolf's limbs as it runs, that he will be transformed into precious energy, that he will race through the wolf's veins, reborn.

Roman kicks the wooden brace away, and he grips the car door handle with his good hand while he prepares the other hand wide with welcome. The wolf already moves like a hurricane confined, nearing the moment when it will become a rush of gray fur. The air is fast in his lungs. Everything drums, drums faster. He hopes that opening the car door will do what he wants: that it will turn everything wild, and the strange heart beating on the wrong side of the window affirms, *It will, it will, it will*. And in the calm moment just before he pulls the handle, he whispers a final command to the wolf far too softly for human ears to perceive.

THE EXORCISE MACHINE

Invention is the mother fucking necessity. But I'll have to figure out how to keep the hammering and drilling and shit quiet, or the landlord's going to get all bitchy again. That first time, yeah, it was pretty much my bad. I normally hold my liquor like a heavyweight, but something about Wild Turkey gets me all rowdy, and I just happened to be in the middle of Turkey-hunting the night my girlfriend Courtney came over to tell me she's breaking up with me for some other guy who actually listens, as she puts it, and who doesn't treat her like a car. I told her that I love my fucking car. Old-school Mustang, 5 Liter V-8, long tube headers, 4.10 gears, enough torque to snap your neck—it's badass. But I didn't smack her or nothing like that—I'm a good guy—all I wanted to know before she ran off with him was the faggot's name, but she knew better than to tell me. You want something done, you got to do it myself, as always. So I started to find out on my own, but I didn't get very far through the phone book that night until things got out of hand. It's embarrassing to get five-o called on you for a domestic dispute when you're home alone. My landlord's one of those fast talkers about lease agreements and disturbances and one-two-three-strikes you're out, but what he didn't understand was that with that second big disturbance, this past Friday, it really wasn't my fault. I got possessed.

So now I'm sitting here scratching my head because the part that's giving me the most trouble is getting the holy water to spray on its own. Mounting all the equipment to my bed is pretty easy since I built my bed frame out of lumber myself, so I've just been using joints and arms that I welded at work up at Drill Co., and I've been bolting them into the wood wherever I need them. At first, for the holy water, I tried to use an empty Windex bottle, and I rigged up my old Christmas toy train engine to rotate a band in a back-and-forth action so it would squeeze the handle and spray across the bed. And it worked too, except that the plastic handle wouldn't pop back out to spray more than once. So I got pissed and threw it across the room. Now I'm thinking about using a fuel injector.

When it first happened, I didn't know what the hell was going on because I didn't think we had earthquakes in Kentucky. But this past Friday my whole room shook me awake, beer bottles falling off my nightstand, cans of paint falling off the shelf and smashing my video games. My bed started shaking and hopping, the headboard popping up, then the foot end, back and forth like that faster and faster until my bed was bucking like the mechanical bull down at Ranch West Bar-B-Q.

And it felt like a big fucking refrigerator on my chest, crushing me into the mattress, but there wasn't actually anything there that I could see. And when I tried to breathe I sounded gut-shot with the way I sucked in air, all sick and wheezing.

Blood started spitting out of my mouth, red specks shooting up into the air and falling back down on my face, and I coughed out a string of foreign words or something like, *Osummamalignispiritus*.

Then I watched my own hands lift above me. I tried to fight them back down—felt just like arm wrestling—but the harder I tried, the more my wrists shook and spazzed-out, and the more my fingers curled back like claws. I watched my hands rip at my favorite motocross T-shirt and scratch at my stomach. My skin burned, and blood pooled around my fingernails—my own fucking hands.

But I couldn't do shit except watch because it had taken over my whole body, except for my feet that I kept kicking into my footboard, but what good does that do?

My bed apparently hopped back far enough that it smashed out the window because glass showered everywhere in a sharp explosion, and everything stopped—totally silent—the whole room deader than my grandma.

I got up and ran to the bathroom, even though I don't know what a bathroom could have done for me at that point. I guess it was just the drinker's toilet-hugging instinct coming out in me. But I noticed in the mirror that whatever had taken over my hands had carved graffiti into my stomach. In spiky letters it said, M-I-N-E. All right, I thought, fuck this dude. He thinks he can come into my apartment and write "mine" on me? Take over my hands? My hands bring me double-and-a-half minimum wage at Drill Co. My hands fixed up a five-hundred-dollar junk Mustang into a street racing Godzilla. I don't care how tough he thinks he is. I watched *The Exorcist*. I got tools. And when he comes back, I'm going to have a nice surprise waiting for his ass.

Now I have to take a break away from working on the holy water sprayer because I realized two things: one, if I'm going to pick a fight with a demon I need some way to smack-talk him. And two, I never actually did watch *The Exorcist*. So I'm in line at the Walmart with my cart full of supplies, flipping through the a tabloid for tips, even though it's all about Bigfoots and Bat-Boy this week, when I get up to the register and realize who the checkout girl is: my girlfriend Courtney.

Obviously, I need to earn back some face and make a good impression, so I say, "I didn't know you were at this register, or I would've gone to the other one."

"Thanks," she says. "You look shitty. Heard you got arrested that one night."

"Nuh-uh. I did not. Who told you that? Your new boyfriend?"

"Police scanner," she says as she belt-feeds my supplies over the beeper.

"Well, I got a new girlfriend," I say. Chicks love to get jealous.

She smirks as she rings up my Collector's Edition of *The Exorcist* DVD and my Ouija Board and says, "Is your new girlfriend a witch?"

Yeah, real funny, but I thought of a better one than that, so I say, "You know what makes me the best street racer in the county, what separates *me* from the men and the boys?"

"That you're too stupid to buckle up?"

"I never forget to buckle up."

"Yes you do," she says. "Sometimes I think my cat's got more sense than you."

"Yeah, well your cat drinks out of the toilet."

She sighs. "Your total is fifty-six eighty."

"Come on. Seriously, know what makes me the best?"

She rolls her eyes and says in a deep voice, "Reaction time. Reaction time."

"No. Reaction time on the pedals. Foot speed. And my feet are so fast that I'll run and have a bunch of girlfriends before you will."

She just stares at me.

I don't think it came out right.

"It's fifty-six eighty," she says.

So I give her a hundred, and after she gives me my change, I high-tail it out of the Walmart because I just gave myself an idea: foot speed.

I've made a lot of headway on my set-up, and now I'm putting on the finishing touches. I'm on the couch, tilting the corner of my mouth up to keep the cigarette smoke out of my eyes so I can watch some documentary about sumo wrestlers where it shows them throwing salt around to scare demons away—bunch of morons. If they want to know what really works, they should watch me: right now I'm duct-taping one end of a garden hose to the mouth of my army surplus gasmask.

There's a knock at the front door. Shit, it better not be the landlord. I didn't even do anything this time. And I only got two strikes on me, even though that second wasn't my fault. I throw my hands up and stomp to the door, open it, and there stands this little black dude with glasses and a tan suit.

I take the cigarette out of my mouth to be polite, and I say, "What do you want? You a lawyer?"

"Hello and good morning," he says like one of those magna-cum-loudly geeks in high school. He hands me this flyer with a drawing of a half-naked guy getting the shit beat out of him. "We want to invite you to celebrate the anniversary of the death of our Lord Jesus Christ."

"Holy fucking shit," I say. "I can't believe it. You Mormons got great timing."

"Actually, we're not Mormon, we belong to the Congregation of Jehovah's Witnesses."

"Come on in. I got something to show you. I need your help on it."

He feints like he is about to come in, then he says, "I *would* like to take the opportunity to talk to you about Jesus Christ."

"Oh, I got something better than Jesus. You'll love it. Come on in. It'll just take a minute."

He steps through the door, so I lead him back. "Get you a beer?" But I don't give him a chance to say *hell yeah* because we're already in the bedroom, so I slap the bedpost and say, "Here she is, my own little exorcist. Almost done." Then I use my hand to push the gas pedals that I rigged up into the footboard. "Look, when I hit this pedal, it clicks down here to turn the tape recorder on. This second pedal starts the automatic air-freshener spray that'll be filled with holy water—okay, I admit, I stole it off the bathroom wall at the Quickstop, but it's all for God's work and shit, right,

Father? This next pedal's actually a clutch from an old Corvette, but what it does is—"

He interrupts me, "What is this supposed to be?"

"It gets demons out of you. I came down with one last week. You deal with them a lot?"

"If you're sincere about this, you should not try to deal with this on your own. Those are the kind of matters that the community and leadership of a church like ourselves are here for."

"Yeah right, me go to a priest? How about next I'll start taking my car to a fucking mechanic, then I'll start paying people to wipe my own ass."

"But, son, the only real way to fight evil is to build a relationship with Jesus."

"Not if you've seen how I do with relationships. Five bucks says Jesus will leave me for some faggot like Courtney did. Come here to the bathroom. I need your help with something." I push the back of his head down as I lead him in there. "Watch out for these ropes and pulleys."

When he sees all the rigging I have on the toilet, he gets all twitchy and starts fiddling with his glasses. "Instead," he says, "I would really like to encourage you to come to our church about all these troubles."

"Okay, what I need you to do is," I say as I take off the toilet tank lid, "I need you to bless all this water real quick."

"We don't do that kind of thing."

"Come on," I say and nudge him with my elbow. "It won't hurt nothing. I really need it to be holy water for everything to work."

"You don't understand."

"I'll make you a deal," I say. "If you bless my water, I'll come do your church stuff for *one* Sunday."

"But it doesn't work like that."

I move to get in between him and the bathroom door. He barely comes up to my chin. "Look, I've been real nice this whole time, and you've pretty much been acting like an asshole." I pop my knuckles. "Let's not have any more trouble. Just bless the fucking water, and we'll call it a day."

He stands still for a moment, his Adam's apple bobbing, then he stretches his skinny little hand out and says, "I bless this toilet."

I slap him on the back. "That wasn't so hard was it? Let me get you a beer." But as I walk back to the fridge, I hear the front door slam shut behind him.

I'm in bed and ready now, all decked out. I'm wearing my leather trench coat because there's no way I could claw through that with just my fingers, and I got my gasmask on. I feel like Darth Vader, except my mask has a big green garden hose running from the mouth of it to the bathroom. But I still bet I look pretty badass lying here.

I got the Ouija board on my lap and I'm using the plastic magnifying glass thingy to spell out one letter at a time, "Come-On-Back-Muth-Er-Fuck-Er. I-Dare-You." But after about a dozen times of doing that, I just spell, "Come-Get-Some" because it's quicker.

Every now and then I spell out stuff that the demon's mom does for two dollars, and after about a half hour, I figure I did enough Ouija smack-talking to get his attention, so I lean up to check my equipment, hitting my nightstand and almost knocking over my big carton of Epsom salt—for the infections I got from those scratches (I'm not about to go to a damned doctor). Then I lie back and wait.

Just as I start to doze off, my bed shakes.

He's back.

Boom—I hit the first gas pedal on the footboard. I hear the tape recorder click, and the static fills the speakers.

My arms curl up, and my head starts twitching side to side like a bird, and I can't stop it.

But blasting in the speakers, I can hear that scene I taped from *The Exorcist*. "The power of Christ compels you! Depart from this child of God!"

My hands fly up to my face, but they're only scratching my gas mask. I stomp footboard gas pedal number two.

Swish—the Quick Stop air freshener starts spraying the holy water I put in there from my blessed toilet. I feel my teeth clack together real hard like I'm trying to chomp through my mask. Now I know I'm winning because when you fight someone, it's always the loser who starts to bite.

The tape keeps blasting, "The power of Christ compels you!" Then after a brief static pause, my I hear my own voice over the speakers reading that thing I got off of Wikipedia: "Therefore I adjure you, unclean spirit, you spectray from Hell, wait, you spect-er from Hell in the name of Jesus Christ of Nazareth to cease your assaults against insert name here. For it is the Lord who condemns you back to the abyss."

Then my body arches up, doing a backbend, and my hands and feet start walking me off the bed like an upside-down spider.

Shit—my pedals—I can't reach them.

My back cracks. I move in circles on my floor, bringing one hand up then slapping it down, one foot up then slapping it down, one by one, all twitchy like those really old black-and-white movies.

I can't so much as even look over at my pedals because my head shakes side-to-side so fast that my brains are smashing inside my skull. The room starts to move far away like a train in a tunnel, and everything grows dark. I lost.

As I slip away, I have one last thought: I should have strapped myself into the bed. I forgot to buckle up.

From a distance, I see my body still spider-walking in circles, but my legs kick over the nightstand, and the whole container of Epsom salt spills over my chest. My body lurches. I zoom super close-up back into myself, stomach and heart and lungs all on fire, screaming.

A gigantic bubble rises from my stomach, up through my throat like I'm puking out another world. It almost dislocates my jaw as it squeezes out of my mouth, filling my gas mask with a thick green cloud. I realize that my body has fallen to the ground—I can move. I lunge to the footboard and slam the final Corvette pedal. The ropes that string across the room and out the door all tense tight. The pulleys squeak. And I hear the bathroom toilet flush.

The green cloud in my mask swirls like a drain out of the mask. The tubing swells, and I watch the bulge slide along the garden hose.

My body is every kind of broken, but I crawl after the moving lump to watch it. I get into the bathroom just after it does, and the green cloud empties out of the hose into the plastic-covered toilet bowl. The fog swirls and swirls with the water, getting thinner as the commode swallows it, then with a gulp gulp gulp it's gone.

It's all gone.

I had all sorts of kick-ass catchphrases ready for this moment, just like the movies, but I fall to the linoleum too hurt to even talk. Anyway, it's enough for me to know that I didn't flush that demon all by his lonesome—I left him a nice little holy floater in there.

It must be noon or something, and I'm still sprawled out on the bathroom floor, just now waking up because someone is pounding on the front door like crazy. I hear yelling too.

"Get out here! I told you three strikes and you're out, buddy!"

The fucking landlord. If he was pissed about all the exorcism noise last night, just wait till he tries to barge in on me on sees all this.

"You hear me in there?" He's rattling the door handle. "Hey, did you change these locks? You changed the locks on my property?"

You bet I did. It's the first thing I do to any rental. The more I listen to him screaming outside, the more I really don't feel like stepping out there just to get evicted face-to-face. I struggle my aching ass up and find my pay-as-you-go cell phone.

And while I'm scrolling through the phone numbers, I'm thinking that it's not that I'm trying to crawl back to her or anything, but after I get kicked out of this place I've got nowhere else to go.

I dial Courtney's number.

I can barely hear her phone ring over the landlord's

pounding and screaming, "Open this door, you bum! I want your ass out today! Three strikes!"

She answers the phone, saying, "Uh, this is a bad time. Can I call you back?"

"Courtney," I say. "It's me."

"I know. But I kinda have a problem right now."

Sometimes I forget how selfish she can be. I say, "I got bigger problems. I'm getting kicked out of my place. You need to let me stay with you for a little while."

"Okay," she says.

That's it. No argument or anything. Something must be wrong.

"What kinda problem is it? Can't your new faggot boyfriend take care of it?"

"He ran out of the apartment screaming. I don't think he's going to be back. It's my cat—"

I can barely hear her over the landlord's bitching outside. I scream at the door, "Shut up! I'm trying to listen to my girlfriend, you asshole!"

She says, "That's sweet."

"What's sweet?"

"Listening to me."

"Courtney, what's the problem?"

She says, "My cat was drinking some green water out of the toilet, and then her head started spinning around backwards. Right now she's walking on the ceiling and talking in some kind of weird language."

"Don't worry," I say. "I know just what to do."

BORGES LIVES IN MY BASEMENT: OR, THERE ARE MORE THINGS

> "There are more things in heaven and earth, Horatio,
> Than are dreamt of in your philosophy."
> —William Shakespeare, *Hamlet*

> "There Are More Things" is also the title of the
> Jorge Luis Borges story that he dedicated
> "to the memory of H.P. Lovecraft."

I didn't have the time to take away from my portfolio to run an errand for someone else, at the library of all places, but Lance was a roommate and a loyal friend, and there was the off-chance that I could wander across some creature-concept designs to steal from old books, so I went. I had to get some good ideas down on paper soon, sketches that the studio guys would finally call original, a true vision.

It was night. Closing time was soon. A few homeless guys woke from the library armchairs and roamed like ghosts. I had grabbed the book Lance wanted, a book on prehistoric whale anatomy for a novel he was writing—I don't know why he couldn't have just researched some diagrams on the Internet—but then I found myself wandering through a labyrinth of aisles that had no orienting signage or numbering. As best as I could tell, it was the third and a half floor, maybe the fourth and a half floor. It wasn't a full floor: no elevator access, no windows. That's where I saw Jorge Luis Borges.

My brain tends to remember images well and faces even better, and I had seen two of his author pics in my college lit book, one in the upper left of the left page, another toward the end of the book in the middle left. Here in the library with me, like his old photos, he had a discoverer's face, half aglow with amazement, an old-world look that reminded me of the elderly version of Bela Lugosi, the Ed Wood years, or at least when Martin Landau played Bela in the Burton film.

It was Borges in the flesh, all right. And I could tell he was already blind by how he felt his way down the aisle of books, fingers crawling across the spines, feet inching forward darkly. I felt that in such a situation I should say something, and I watched him, trying to think of some impressive or profound statement, but I noticed the little can-shaped roll-stool in his way. I said, "Watch out!"

He startled, straightening tall and fanning both arms out on either aisle, searching around with his face as if to hear my location, or to sniff me out. I felt guilt for having used the idiom *watch out*, a thoughtless insensitivity toward his condition, but then I felt a far worse guilt for not having known enough about Borges before this moment. I couldn't seem to remember any details about his fiction or poetry that we read in college, and I hadn't touched any of his non-fiction, though I remembered a cool-looking monster on the cover of a book of his about imaginary beings—a thick-headed sphinx-pegasus with a peacock tail. Regardless, I just knew that Borges had to be full of original ideas since we did have to study him. I should have at least had a sense of his biography, or of when he had died, or something about his impact on the history of literature, but I was blank-page ignorant. I felt like an ass.

I neared him, warning while I did, "I'm walking closer to you." I decided to come clean first thing about my ignorance, just in case his blindness made him particularly apt at detecting bullshit. "Sorry," I said, "I know you're Jorge Luis Borges, and it's an honor to run into you, but I have to admit that I don't know much about you, literature-history-wise. And when we did read your work, I was kind of into other things at the time." Dark Horse Comics, Image, Marvel, lots of Jim Lee, some old-school Jack Kirby, anything by Mike Mignola—those four-color panels flashed through my brain as fast as shuffling cards. "I guess I did pleasure-reading more than college-reading. But we did study you in a literature class."

He reset himself into a comfortable slouch and smiled. He said to me, "I have tried to disregard as much as possible the history of literature. When my students asked me for a bibliography, I told them, 'A bibliography is unimportant— after all. Shakespeare knew nothing of Shakespearean criticism. Why not study the texts directly? If you like the book, fine; if you don't, don't read it. The idea of compulsory reading is absurd; it's only worthwhile to speak of compulsory happiness.'" [1]

I liked that. And that's exactly what I was in need of, some compulsory happiness. This upcoming deadline to submit my portfolio, my creature-concept designs, my opportunity to get a real job with an fx studio—this was my last shot. There were only so many places in this industry to get rejected. My unemployment checks were going to dry up soon. I hadn't opened my credit card statements in months. My girlfriend left me for a guy who sells smartphones to other guys who already have them. I had even considered reading up on how to operate the pistol I kept up in the closet. And while it was great to have my friend Lance helping out by living in my basement unit, I figured it wouldn't be long before his novel took off and he'd be gone. To top it off, I've been crumpling up page after page of my designs because I can hear the studio guys in my head already: *We've seen that monster before.* Or, *that's just this mixed with that. A bear with an owl,* or *a shark with a bird,* and so on. *What we need is something original.* As if that exists. I needed compulsory happiness, all right. And I needed some help with that.

So I asked Borges about his take on monster-making. "If you don't mind my asking, do you think it's even possible to draw an entirely new monster design? Like a really original vision? It seems to me, even back in ancient times people just accidentally came up with monsters just because they didn't know any better and ended up misunderstanding regular animals. I only ask because of the cover on that book of yours, the one with the human head on the horse body."

"The Centaur?" [2] he said, still seeming a little unsure about me. Or maybe he didn't know the book cover I was referring to, the sphinx-pegasus.

"Yeah, let's take the centaur for example," I said. "Like the first time ancient people saw a guy riding a horse, they just mistook it for a monster, and there you go. No real original vision, just a mix-and-match accident."

"But. . ." he said, "the Greeks did know the horse. It seems more likely that the Centaur is a deliberately drawn image." [3]

"So you think it's possible for an artist to deliberately come up with an entirely new monster, and it could stick around in people's heads? Maybe for thousands of years?"

"I think it is," [4] he said.

And with the way he said it, the way he canted *I think it is*, with a kind of scoffing obviousness that didn't come off as much rude as it did patient—patient with my youth, patient with my ignorance, like an old magician—I think I was immediately convinced. If I brought him home with me and had him coaching me, I could churn out a portfolio that would blow minds and shake the world. He surely wouldn't be much trouble to keep around since he had been dead for so long. So I went for it.

"I tell you what," I said. "I'd really love it if you came and lived with me for a while. It's not much, but it's a warm place to sleep and some decent food to eat. I have lots of vintage movies from, you know—" I didn't want to say from his lifetime "—from your era. I feel like you could really help me out with some ideas I'm trying to get going."

He didn't seem immediately against it. But he said, "I would like to give you fair warning of what to expect—or, rather what not to expect from me." He rubbed the swollen knuckles of his hands. "The truth is that I have no revelations to offer." [5]

Of course I didn't believe his humility, but rather than argue, I just said, "I don't mind. Come anyway. It'll be a nice change for me. Besides, I'm sure I haven't given you the respect you deserve, the writer you are and all. If I drew out some of the monsters that you tell me about, I could do proper justice to your writing."

"To do justice to a writer," he said, "one must be unjust to others." [6]

"Maybe so, but I guess I don't care anymore," I said. "Other writers haven't helped me out any, and it's time I focused on some artistic vision of my own. I have you here with me now, and you can help me come up with a monster that is—" an impressive word wasn't coming to me—a monster that is what?—but then I saw it written on the cover of the prehistoric whale book that I held "—a monster that is unfathomable!"

He wrinkled his brow.

I was excited, already feeling inspiration for the first time in months. I took him carefully by the arm and led him through the aisles, looking to find an emergency exit so we could escape from the library without anyone seeing us or asking questions to which the answers, at this point, would be too confusing for a stranger to comprehend and too insulting to say in front of a great man like Borges. And sneaking out meant that Lance wouldn't have to worry about returning the book I had picked up for him, though I wasn't sure how I would explain all this to him.

I wanted Borges to wait for me outside the house while I broke the news about him moving in with us, just in case Lance reacted poorly at first. I didn't know exactly what poor reaction to expect out of Lance, but he tended to be more skeptical and conservative than I, making my proposition to let Borges move in with us a shaky one.

Since it was sleeting, I had Borges wait in the cubby of

the front porch. Also, from inside, I could see him through the window, and I wanted to keep him in the corner of my eye. I wasn't exactly sure if he was the kind of old man who might wander off, but since I had found him all alone and wandering, I assumed he was in fact that kind.

I yelled down the basement stairs to Lance, telling him that I got his library book but that I needed to talk to him. My plan was simple: tell him the truth, list the benefits of having Borges move in, and hope that he would agree. I was certain that, given a moment to consider the magnitude, the possibilities, he would agree.

Lance hopped up the stairs, skipping an occasional step, asking me what was up.

"You have to promise not to tell anyone," I said.

Lance gestured toward the window at Borges outside, who was turning his head in the yellow light of the porch bulb, listening to the sleet. "Who's that?"

"I found him in the library. It's Jorge Luis Borges, the famous writer. He's going to move in with us. He's from Argentina, and he wrote all kinds of stuff, and he's an expert on monsters."

"I know who Borges is," Lance said. "And he's dead."

"Don't say that," I said, looking back to make sure that Borges hadn't heard that through the door.

"He died in the '80s. That's not him."

"It is him. Just look at him," I said. "If you promise to be cool about it, I'll let you talk to him, and you can ask him anything you want. Then you'll see. But you have to promise to help me keep him a secret."

"I have no idea if that guy looks like Borges or not, and I don't care. This is nutty, man. The pressure's getting to you." Lance took the library book out of my hand and flipped through pages. He let a centerfold fall open that showed an anatomical map of some atrocious version of a sperm whale, its skeleton, its muscles, its nasty teeth. He turned away from me toward the basement. "Just give that guy some food or liquor or whatever he's here for, and send him away. And get some rest, man. Jesus."

"No, Lance," I said. My stomach quivered, but I was determined to have Borges move in no matter what it took. "He's staying. He's going to live here. I don't want to be an asshole about it, but it's my house."

Lance faced me again, somehow amused. "You think he's going to help you with your portfolio, don't you? For the job?"

"Yeah, and who better?" I said. "They want monsters from me, don't they? They want real vision."

"I don't want to have to say it, but you're not going to get that job," he said. "You have to know that. You haven't had a single real vision in your whole life. Listen, you're a good sketcher and a good inker, but you're not a prophet, man. You're not John the Revelator. I'm trying to look out for you, and I've got to tell you that this is getting real crazy. I can't let you keep it up."

I tossed up my hands and tried to yell, but I didn't know what to say. I couldn't believe he would say that. I could have real vision. I would prove it.

Apparently, he could tell I was upset. "Listen, listen," he said, softening his tone a little. "I'm sure you can get some kind of job in the industry, and you'll do fine, but you have to be realistic. I've seen you do this before. You get a glimpse of something great that's way out of your league, and then you totally obsess over it. It never goes well."

"When have I ever done that?"

"You're single again, aren't you? You're unemployed again. Look, if you're too uncomfortable telling that guy he has to leave, I'll do it." Lance started toward the front door.

I blocked his path. He was going to be mean to Borges. He was just going to hurt his feelings like he did to me, and while I could take it, I didn't know if Borges could, not given his odd condition. I couldn't have Lance tossing him out in the cold. I said, "You're not talking to him. And he's not leaving. You are."

"You can't seriously be kicking me out."

"You're either for me or against me on this, and you're against me, so you're out." My voice sounded stormy, and

I liked it. I had never before stood my ground like that. Maybe I had just needed someone else to defend. I would be damned if I let anyone else run Borges off. He was with me now. Borges and I were in this together. We would draw forth a monster together. I told Lance, "Leave through the back door in the utility room. Don't even look at Borges anymore. I'm not going to say it twice."

"You know what? I don't need this." He tossed the book down on the couch and then pointed close to my face. "You know what you are? You're an Ahab, man. Yeah, you keep chasing after something you don't even understand, and you're going to destroy yourself."

"If I'm Ahab," I said, "then you're. . ." I wanted to turn his reference back around on him, and I was trying to recall the name of that prophet that Ahab fought with in the Bible. Was it Ezekiel or Elijah or something? The name wasn't clear to me, but I did remember an old etch-style illustration of the scene with a chariot in the background. "Then you're that prophet, the one who. . ."

"You know which Ahab I meant, you freak. You're not even making any sense. I'm out of here."

"Then you're overboard," I said. Although I was feeling the power of the moment, I knew I was terrible with the witty comebacks, and I knew that one was lame. Lance was always good with them, good at talking people down, but he even admitted once that it was a fake skill of his—a sleight of hand—so I knew not to take anything cruel he said to heart.

But I didn't expect him to leave just like that, without another word, without even collecting anything he owned from the basement, and yet he did, right out the back door. He had other friends, lots of them, so he probably just went to stay with one of them. I was suspicious for a moment whether he had planned to move out soon anyway, but, on second thought, I was sure he would come back in a day or so, and we would patch things up over a case of beer, and I would show him all the inspired art and monster designs that Borges would help me with. It would be fine.

Until then, I had to make Borges feel at home in the basement, and I had to get him talking about monsters.

It wasn't long before I grew a little annoyed with Borges. In the basement I had prepared his cot, got a space heater ready, and brought down a lamp that he didn't even really require. In order for him to have something near the cot to set stuff on, or to reach out to, or to lean on, I even dragged a small dresser down the stairs. It was a bad decision to try to go down backward under the dresser, the steep wooden steps whining under the weight, the pipe railing loose like a stick in sand. I thought I would fall through, tap my skull on the concrete like a nutshell, and be dead in the basement with Borges for eternity.

But I didn't die, or even fall, and I had gone to a lot of trouble to build him a cozy little dorm. I also brought down my laptop to watch the original *King Kong* with him, one of the masterworks of American cinema. I knew he couldn't *watch it* watch it, but I tend to talk through films, so I described most of the shots. Borges remembered a lot of it anyway, as he told me, from when he had seen it during its original release in theaters in Argentina, back when he had sight.

Here was my basic plan: We'd watch the film, and then we would say wonderful things about it over a cheap bottle of cognac that I had, and then King Kong would get him talking about other great monsters, summoning all that mythical knowledge and all those original ideas that I could translate into art for my portfolio.

It didn't work. Borges hated King Kong.

"How can you hate King Kong?" I said.

He said, "A monkey forty feet tall—" [7]

"He's forty-five," I said. "Forty five-feet tall." I knew my King Kong. I owned the special edition DVD.

"Forty-five," he continued, "may have some obvious charms, but—" [8]

"But what?" I said. "Willis O'Brien, the guy who animated it, he created a real monster for the first time in the history of all humanity. Audiences back then hadn't

ever seen anything like that. Kong was climbing on
buildings that people in the theater really knew. The
cinematographer was a genius, and O'Brien summoned a
real, full-blooded ape up from primordial chaos!"

Borges paused and then started again with distinct
punctuation, emphasis on the pick-up words, like a man
delivering a lecture that ought not to have been interrupted.
"King Kong is no full-blooded ape but rather a rusty,
desiccated machine whose movements are downright clumsy.
His only virtue, his height, did not impress the cinematographer, who persisted in photographing him from above
rather than from below—the wrong angle, as it neutralizes
and even diminishes the ape's overpraised stature." [9]

"Overpraised stature? He'd rip this whole house down,
and then he'd scoop out this basement like a grapefruit
and squish us into a bloody mess! He's massive. Look at
him." I knew I was pointing at the DVD menu screen of
an image of Kong fighting a wickedly strange-looking T-
rex that Borges could not see, but that didn't make me
any less right.

"He is actually hunchbacked and bowlegged, attributes
that serve only to reduce him in the spectator's eye. To
keep him from looking the least bit extraordinary, they
make him do battle with far more unusual monsters and
have him reside in caves of false cathedral splendor, where
his infamous size again loses all proportion." [10]

"This is unreal," I said. "I'd love to see what kind of
monsters could possibly impress you if King Kong—the
greatest American monster—is just a little hunchback
monkey to you. How big does a monster have to be?" My
head was hot and heavy. It was the cognac and the lack of
sleep, mostly the cognac, which had gotten me standing
and slapping the cinderblock basement wall while I talked
without thinking clearly. "Put King Kong in his place, why
don't you? What do you got that's better? I'm ready to see
it. I'm here in a basement with a guy who came back from
the dead just so I can come up with a monster, so show me
a real monster!"

"I timidly point out this monstrousness to my interlocutor." [11] Then he said nothing else. He took his cane and sat tapping the floor with it, with ticks like a waiting clock, probably indicating as politely as possible that he was ready to be left alone for the night.

I sat back down and wished I hadn't said what I said. I stayed silent for a while and kept swigging cognac. Then I offered an apology for my rude and aggressive manner—blaming fatigue and liquor—and I wished him a good-night with a promise that I would bring him breakfast early in the morning. I left him down in the basement, taking the bottle of cognac with me. I sat on my bed, drinking and sketching, coming up with one junk design after another. I could have cried. In the long mirror facing me on the back of my bedroom door, I looked pathetic and creepy, crouched up on the bed like the little demon in Fuseli's painting *The Nightmare*. I threw a dirty towel over the door to cover the mirror, and flopped back on the bed, giving up for the night, but just as I was drifting off, I got an idea for what to try next with Borges.

"Tell me about your nightmares, Borges."

It was mid-morning, and I had come back from the store, brewed some Columbian coffee, cooked some bacon, even cut up a grapefruit for him. I brought it down to the basement on a baking sheet, which was the closest thing I owned to a silver platter. He had apparently found a bathroom kit that Lance had left behind, and he was clipping his fingernails. He let the clippings fly onto the floor.

"The nightmare," [12] he said as if he were making formal introductions. "Dreams are the genus; nightmares the species." [13]

"Exactly. Tell me about what scares you most in your dreams." I laid out his breakfast on the little dresser and then sat myself on the floor, away from his fingernail clippings, with my sketch pad in my lap, my Faber-Castell 9000 pencils at the ready.

He said, "I have two nightmares which often become confused with one another. I have the nightmare of the labyrinth, which—" [14]

"Wait a second," I said, stopping him so I could turn on the lamp for better lighting, also realizing that I wouldn't be able to do much monster-design work using something like a labyrinth as inspiration. "Okay," I said as I sat back down, "so the labyrinth is one, but what's your other nightmare?"

He found the coffee with his hand, sipped it, seemed disappointed, and went back to clipping his nails. "My other nightmare is that of the mirror. The two are not distinct, as it only takes two facing mirrors to construct a labyrinth." [15]

"Mirrors scare me too," I said, feeling quickly enthusiastic about the idea. "I had to cover up my bedroom mirror last night!"

"In the dream of the mirror, another vision appears. . . the mask. Masks have always scared me. I see myself reflected in the mirror, but the reflection is wearing a mask. I am afraid to pull the mask off, afraid to see my real face, which I imagine to be hideous." [16]

I was sketching like mad, liking what I saw for the first time in untold weeks. "This is good. This is good," I said.

Borges went on some more about some other writers, Coleridge and Petronius and whatnot, but I was deep into my lead, deaf with inspiration, possessed by ideas. I was filling up pages of stylized South-Pacific masks with cannibal teeth and even more pages of a mask design styled like a Victorian mirror. Maybe the concept was that the South-Pacific mask needs to be fed raw human flesh. Maybe it gives the wearer power when it gets fed, but maybe after the food passes the mask the wearer has to eat it all too. Maybe the Victorian mirror-mask steals the face of whomever it reflects. Masks always work for studios doing horror movies—Michael Myers, Jason, the *Scream* guy— and the cinematographers always squeeze in shots of seeing the killer in the mirror. Why hadn't I thought of using something in my sketches that actually creeped me out, like mirrors?

What I needed was a model to keep the inspiration flowing. I needed to stare into some mirrors and make exaggerated faces in them like masks. I told Borges this, and I let him know that he was free to wander around inside the house as he pleased but not to leave the house at all. He wouldn't be safe out there in my neighborhood, around the crazies and the thugs, around people who couldn't appreciate him like I did.

As I was on my way up the stairs, he warned me about seeing a fish in the mirror.

"A fish?" I said.

"The Fish," he said, either repeating himself for emphasis or distinguishing a special fish—a capital *F* fish—from all other fish. Either way, he was not happy about it at all. He had turned serious. "An elusive, gleaming creature that no one had ever touched but that many people believed they had seen in the depths of mirrors." [17]

I told him that I didn't know anything about that Fish but that I would find out more later and that at the moment I needed to get to work and that he was free to adjust the thermostat to whatever made him comfortable.

He was slow with his words now, dark with his tone. "The first to awaken shall be the Fish," he said. He had stopped clipping his nails. He stood, facing the cinderblock wall, doing nothing with his hands, blind but seeing something. I didn't like it. "In the depths of the mirror, we shall perceive a faint, faint line, and the color of the line will not resemble any other." [18]

I had never before imagined what having visions or revelations actually looked like to an outside observer like me who was seeing the person having them. It was disturbing, like when a pet or some kind of animal is bristling and growling at an empty corner in an old house, you being the only one not seeing what there is to fear.

I told myself that whatever was going on with Borges at the moment was private—I was sure he had worries of his own—so I left him down in the basement, still talking to himself. I desperately needed to get to work while that ever-fleeting inspiration was still with me. I needed a full day of sketching, and I needed to put in an all-nighter on top of that.

I pulled all the mirrors in the house off their hinges and brackets, pulled them out of the drawers, even gathered some reflective glasses and bottles, and I surrounded my drafting table with them. I quickly realized that the morning sun coming in through the slits in the window blinds caught my eye through one mirror or another, so I had to take the time to pull out every sheet and coat and towel I owned and cover every window. I stood the couch up against the front door to block the light from the gaps along its seal. It was so dark that I needed to turn on some lights, but none that would catch my mirrors directly, so I turned on all the flashlights that I had and angled them away from me. A few candles helped too. I had no idea what time it was when I finally got to sit down and grab a pencil, but once I did and started making monster faces in the mirrors, it was all the inspiration I needed, and I lost myself in the work, hours and hours of glorious blur.

The pilot light to the gas heater must have been snuffed out hours prior to my coming to, to my awaking out of a daze. My arms and legs shivered, and by the dull light I could see my breath. At some point during the drawing, and the intermittent sleep—against my own will—over my drafting table, and the staring deep into the mirrors, my nose had apparently bled on some of my best designs. It wouldn't matter much. The designs were good, and there were piles of them: masks and mirror-creatures and more masks.

Also I had apparently begun drawing parts of a fish, a big one. It was so big that it would never fit on a single page. I hadn't remembered specifically drawing those, but I did, and I couldn't quit looking back over them, using the tips of my numb fingers to piece them together at the corners in different combinations, trying to get a sense of what the whole fish would look like in a single vision.

I guessed it was about one in the morning. All but one of the flashlights had died, but the candles were still bright. The mirrors looked black beyond the hints of my face reflected in them.

That's when I saw the faint, faint line.

It showed up in the mirror that was on my left, the one I had taken off the bathroom medicine cabinet. The faint, faint line, it was something effable only by analogy. It was like it had a color, a compromise the perception of the brain might make between a spider and the rings of Saturn. The faint, faint line was like the slit of a closed eye, a nearly closed eye, like an animal dreaming. And I looked into the slit of that eye to get a glimpse of what was on the other side. I looked hard. My nose touched the mirror, and it was cold. I held my breath so I wouldn't frost it over. I thought my eyes might lose focus that close, but they didn't. It was just taking time for the image to sharpen.

And the image did sharpen.

I saw floating in a great deep. The line in the mirror didn't open, but I saw into it, and I saw floating in a great deep, hints of a vast fish.

I must have stopped breathing for I don't know how long because I found myself coming back to consciousness on the floor. The room was dizzy, and the faint line in the mirror was gone. I picked myself up and checked all of the mirrors, but it was gone.

I rushed down the stairs to ask Borges about it, yelling as I went. But he was gone too.

I ran back upstairs and checked the front door, checked the rooms, yelling for him, and then I checked the back door in the utility room. It was cracked open.

This was bad. He could run into anybody out there, crazy people. He could leave forever. He had to tell me about the Fish. I had seen a glimpse of it. I needed to see it again. I needed to see all of it. He had to tell me how.

Outside, I saw him just past the back lot, in the alley,

where the street lamp just barely reached. He was talking to a couple of thugs—baggy clothes, weaving heads, flicking hands—and they were laughing, and he was laughing.

I couldn't have that. They weren't capable of understanding the things Borges and I could see.

Back inside, with the last working flashlight, I found the pistol case in my bedroom closet, opened it, and removed the piece. I had no idea if the thing was loaded; I just knew that you pointed it and squeezed the trigger when you had to. I went out back toward the alley and yelled at the thugs to back away from Borges, to leave him alone and get lost.

It took them a moment to see that I was pointing the pistol at them. I think they were smoking weed right next to him. He didn't need that. He needed to be clear-headed. The thugs said, "What the hell, dog?" and they called me crazy.

I repeated myself as I neared them. They didn't stick around.

There was a parked car nearby, in the grass to the side of the alley, and it looked like Lance's car. I had trouble remembering the image of his car for sure—all I could think of was the Fish—but I was pretty sure it was his, so he must have been staying somewhere nearby to spy on me. He was probably waiting for a chance to take Borges away from me. He probably called the cops. I should have never let him know that I had found Borges. But I knew I could scare Lance off if I left him a message, showing him that I was deadly serious. I used the butt of the pistol to smash out the driver's side window so he would know I was to be left alone, that Borges and I were to be left alone, and the thugs would know too, and the cops too.

The car had an alarm, which started blaring, and lights came on in neighbors' windows.

I grabbed Borges by the arm and led him back inside the house, accidentally smearing some blood from a cut on my hand onto his coat. "What were you saying to those guys? What were you talking about?" I was worried they had been mean to him or crude with him. I was worried he told them about the Fish.

"The art of verbal abuse," he said. "The middle finger and a show of tongue. . .'Dog' is another very general term of insult." [19]

"You shouldn't talk to those guys. You shouldn't talk to anybody out here. They're dangerous." I pulled Borges to hurry him with me down the basement steps. It was a deep freeze down there, the cold coming in waves through the cinder-blocks. He was moving slow, sliding his feet rather than picking them up, but we didn't have time for that. I had seen the vast Fish, had seen it in the mirror. Borges had to tell me more.

He had seemed amused since I found him talking with the thugs, not at all gloomy and nightmarish as when I had last left him in the basement. He was singing a poem when I sat him down on his cot:

> *Veinticinco palillos*
> *Tiene una silla.*
> *Quieres que te la rompa*
> *En las costillas?* [20]

I went back up the stairs to secure the basement door, asking him what he was saying, what those words meant, what was the translation, whether they were ancient.

He said:

> "Twenty-five sticks
> Makes a chair.
> Would you like me to break it
> Over your ribs?" [21]

"That's got nothing to do with it, with the Fish," I said. From the inside of the door I shut it, locked it, and used the pistol to hammer the doorstop in the gap at the bottom to keep it wedged shut in the event that Borges figured out how to unlock it. In case I passed out again, down here in the basement, I couldn't have him wandering back outside.

Then I got close to his face and said, "Tell me more about the Fish. Tell me everything."

For a moment he kept that closed-eyed, pleasant look,

but I knew that it was just a mask of his, because what I said had begun to sink in. His smile faded. He was getting back to the Borges that had scared me.

"That's right," I said. "I saw it. I saw it upstairs, a glimpse of it. I passed out but I saw a glimpse through the faint line in the mirror. It was vast. It was terrible and vast."

He lay down on the cot, now as serious as I was. He crossed his hands on his chest, and his voice sounded dead. "People speak not of the Fish." [22]

"But you did. You brought it up. You brought it here with you. You brought it to me." I knelt by his ear as if I were praying into it, my breath misting his skin. "Why didn't you stay dead, Borges? What did you see over there? Tell me about the Fish. Tell me what it is."

"The Leviathan," [23] he said. "The Bahamut. . .a Fish that floats in a bottomless sea." [24]

Someone was knocking upstairs now, knocking on the front door.

"What about it?" I said. I knew somehow that we were running out of time, that others would try to stop us, that creation would conspire against me now that I was seeing through it. "What is the Bahamut? What about it?" I didn't know the right questions to ask.

"A vacant god reeling in the barren centuries of the eternity 'before.'" [25]

"What does that mean? Before what? Before God?"

They knocked more.

"So immense and resplendent is the Bahamut that human eyes cannot bear to look upon it. All the seas of the earth, placed in one of the nostrils of its nose, would be no more than a grain of mustard in the midst of the desert." [26]

The knocking continued. I couldn't have anyone interrupting this. I flicked on my flashlight and turned off the basement lamp, knocking us into near darkness. I helped Borges up quickly and dragged him with me to hide under the basement stairs. I hit my head on the wood underneath the steps. There wasn't much space under there, but what we were on to was bigger than the universe.

I could tell there was yelling outside now, and they beat loudly on the front door with their bodies or their clubs or something, but they wouldn't find me and Borges down here, not if we kept our talking to a whisper.

I muffled the beam of my flashlight under my shirt, letting me see by the faintest glow, and I said softly, "If I keep looking for the Bahamut in the mirror, will I get to see it again? Will I get to see all of it?"

Borges kept his eyes closed as he huddled and shivered. I hadn't seen him shiver before. "Isa—Jesus—was allowed to see the Bahamut, and when this gift was bestowed upon him he fell down in a swoon, and did not awake from the swoon that had come upon him for three days." [27]

"But I'm different, right? Human eyes can't bear it, but I'm a visionary, right? It was almost revealed to me. What would happen if I saw all of it?"

"Nothingness," he said. "As if blasted by a lightless fire." [28]

"Tell me, tell me the truth," I said. "If I look hard again, will I get to see it? Can I awaken it?" I was holding him close by the shoulders, like clinging to a pine box floating in an endless ocean.

"The first to awaken will be the Fish. . . Then, other forms will begin to awaken . . . they will break through the barriers." [29] He was turning his face away from me, and I didn't want him to. He was as scared as I was.

"Is it already awake? Is that why you're here? Is it already awake?" I said. I was shaking. "Oh, God! Is it true? Has it now awoken?"

His eyes opened, and I saw my reflection in them. And in that reflection, I saw the Bahamut, and the Bahamut saw me.

The sources of Borges's dialogue in this story, all quoted from his nonfiction:

[1] *Seven Nights*, page 81
[2] *The Book of Imaginary Beings*, page 45
[3] *The Book of Imaginary Beings*, page 46
[4] *Seven Nights*, page 27
[5] *This Craft of Verse*, page 1
[6] *Borges: Selected Non-Fictions*, page 411
[7] *Borges: Selected Non-Fictions*, page 146
[8] *Borges: Selected Non-Fictions*, page 146
[9] *Borges: Selected Non-Fictions*, page 146
[10] *Borges: Selected Non-Fictions*, page 146
[11] *Borges: Selected Non-Fictions*, page 205
[12] *Seven Nights*, page 32
[13] *Seven Nights*, page 26
[14] *Seven Nights*, page 32
[15] *Seven Nights*, page 33
[16] *Seven Nights*, page 33
[17] *The Book of Imaginary Beings*, page 18
[18] *The Book of Imaginary Beings*, pages 18 - 19
[19] *Borges: Selected Non-Fictions*, page 87
[20] *Borges: Selected Non-Fictions*, page 89
[21] *Borges: Selected Non-Fictions*, page 89
[22] *The Book of Imaginary Beings*, page 19
[23] *The Book of Imaginary Beings*, page 127
[24] *The Book of Imaginary Beings*, page 25
[25] *Borges: Selected Non-Fictions*, page 131
[26] *The Book of Imaginary Beings*, page 26
[27] *The Book of Imaginary Beings*, page 26
[28] *Borges: Selected Non-Fictions*, page 134
[29] *The Book of Imaginary Beings*, pages 19 – 20

JESUS VS. THOR

Now it came to pass, under the sign of Pisces, that a vision was opened & was given. & Behold:

Along the red & cloudy wastes of Jupiter marched an army & their number was one-hundred forty-four thousand & each soldier brandished an unblemished spear & wore a vestment of bronze & each grew a narrow beard like unto a pillar of stone & each soldier upon his forehead did two names gleam like fire & these two names were

יהוה & ישוע

Each soldier was a virgin & was angry.

The army of one-hundred forty-four thousand did clutch their spears and sing a hymn mighty unlike any hymn & it was New to their Lord and all Lords.

Thus did they provoke a jealousy, a terrible jealousy.

The red & cloudy wastes of Jupiter did splash aside to a racing chariot. Two black goats pulled the chariot & their names were Tooth-Gnasher & Gap-Tooth. Aloft in the chariot stood a mighty figure who was called Ása-Thór & his beard was like unto a fiery mane of a lion & iron gauntlets weighed on his mighty hands & a belt of strength did skirt his waist like unto a fortress wall & raised above his head he held a horrid hammer which was wicked, which was ancient, upon which were engraved three terrible secrets which no god could decipher & all who are well informed of this hammer call it only Mjölnir.

Then Ása-Thór did speak with his mighty voice:

"By what authority does this army sing a New praise where mine ears may hear it? For there will be trouble!"

Then the black goats Tooth-Gnasher & Gap-Tooth chomped their jaws like thunder & Ása-Thór rode without fear through the center of the army of one-hundred forty-four thousand & he bore down on them with cutting speed & he swung Mjölnir across their ranks & the heads of the army of one-hundred forty-four thousand did toss like unto a reaping of grain & did splatter like unto grapes of the vine. & Ása-Thór chomped one of their heads with his mighty teeth for show.

The song of the army of one-hundred forty-four thousand did stop & only did they wail and flee. But Ása-Thór chased them in his chariot for sport & smashed their heads & he laughed & the laugh of Ása-Thór did sound as this:

"Hor hor hor hor hor hor hor hor hor hor hor hor hor hor hor hor hor hor hor hor hor hor hor hor hor hor hor hor hor hor hor! Hor!"

And it was then that the army of one-hundred forty-four thousand, which was now the army of forty-eight thousand six-hundred twenty-one, did stop fleeing & grow silent. Likewise did Ása-Thór furrow his brow & become silent.

The red & cloudy wastes of Jupiter were disturbed & stirred because of the massacre of the army of forty-eight thousand six-hundred twenty-one. Through the bloody mist strode a strange shape. It did hobble on four hooves & did bleed from the neck like unto a river & it became clear to all that it was the Lamb.

& the Lamb was a terrible sight to behold. Seven crooked horns did protrude from its skull & seven blank eyes did scatter its face & dark blood did cake its torn wool & all who are well informed of this Lamb know that it had been slaughtered. Yet it hobbled toward Ása-Thór.

& the army of forty-eight thousand six-hundred twenty-one did call its name:

"Yeshua Mshicha! Yeshua bin Yahweh!"

Then did Ása-Thór snort his nostrils & hurl Mjölnir at the Lamb. Mjölnir gleamed like lightning as it tumbled across the red & cloudy wastes of Jupiter & it crashed into the skull of the Lamb & shattered two of its horns & put out three of its eyes & snapped its neck to its shoulder & cleaved its skull & the Lamb fell to its side.

& the Lamb was dead.

Then did Ása-Thór step down from his chariot with much pleasure & he did pat the heads of his two goats Tooth-Gnasher and Gap-Tooth & with his iron gauntlets he did lift corpses by the number of nine at a time in each hand & did pile them so as to make a pyre to commemorate his glory.

The army of forty-eight thousand six-hundred twenty-one watched in horror & prayed for their destroyed soldiers.

Ása-Thór did pile the corpses in a circle that was eighty-two cubits wide & did throw the corpses atop each other until the pile was three-hundred fifty-nine cubits high & all who are well informed of this tower of corpses know that it was tall & vast & terrible. Then did Ása-Thór behold his labors and speak:

"The tips of Yggdrasil are challenged by this heavy work!"

The last corpse to be pilled atop the tower of corpses was that of the Lamb, but as Ása-Thór strode near the Lamb, the Lamb did wobble to its feet.

The neck of the Lamb was still broken to its side & the horns of the Lamb were still shattered & the eyes of the Lamb were still put out & the neck of the Lamb did still bleed as a river, yet the Lamb stood.

This did greatly anger Ása-Thór & he spoke:

"This greatly angers me!"

& the countenance of Ása-Thór did seem to grow like a thunderhead & Ása-Thór clutched the Lamb by the wool with his iron fingers & spun his feet in a violent circle &

became a whirlwind & released the Lamb & the Lamb did fly far out of sight across the red & cloudy wastes of Jupiter.

But Ása-Thór saw that in his palm which had clutched the thick wool of the Lamb there were scattered wax crumbs of a broken seal. Ása-Thór licked them off his gauntlet & spit them out again because the taste did not please him.

Then did cry out the army of forty-eight thousand six-hundred twenty-one:

"Behold! The White Horse approacheth!"

& there rode forth a White Horse upon which sat a White Rider who held a long White Bow & who wore a tall White Crown & who wore a White Veil over his face & who did sing in a voice as beautiful as that of a maiden:

"I come forth conquering & to conquer! I come forth conquering & to conquer! I come forth conquering & to conquer!"

At this, Ása-Thór did not stoop to retrieve Mjölnir for he was jolly at the harm he would do & he ran forth toward the rider at cutting speed & his feet did quake the red & cloudy wastes of Jupiter & he spread his arms & did speak:

"That I should embrace this conqueror!"

Straightaway did the White Rider upon the White Horse & Ása-Thór clash so that the heavens did rumble. Ása-Thór pressed against the White Horse breast upon breast & did clasp his iron gauntlets at the rump of the White Horse & did lift the White Horse & squeeze it terribly.

The White Rider nocked a thin White arrow & pulled his long White bow & shot it down at the face of Ása-Thór like unto a beam of light.

Ása-Thór dropped the White Horse from his grip & clutched his eyes & screamed out of his throat & the scream of Ása-Thór did sound as this:

"Yie yeeeeeeeeeeeeeeeeeeeeeeeeeeeeeeeeeeeeeeeeeeeeee!"

It was then that the river of blood that was left from the neck of the Lamb did pool at the base of the tower of corpses since they did weigh down the red & cloudy wastes of Jupiter like unto a stretched web of cloth. The corpses

began to twitch and splash in the blood of the Lamb &
the corpses at the bottom of the tower of corpses drank
the blood of the Lamb deeply & like unto a fountain the
blood of the Lamb flowed upward through the tower for
they were One. The tower of corpses began to sway and
groan. & one by one the corpse arms which brandished
spears did stretch out at every side of the tower of corpses.
Feet of the corpses stood at the base to lift the tower of
corpses & it was like unto a tall nation of tight dead & the
thousands of indignant eyes did look toward Ása-Thór.

& the tower of corpses lurched toward Ása-Thór.

& the army of forty-eight thousand six-hundred twenty-
one fell into ranks behind the White Rider upon the White
Horse. & the White Rider sang for a volley of spears toward
Ása-Thór.

& they were tossed. The flock of spears climbed high
& blackened the heavens & tilted & rained upon the back
of Ása-Thór. Every spear of the army of forty-eight
thousand six-hundred twenty-one did pierce Ása-Thór &
his back was like unto a thick forest.

Ása-Thór stumbled to the selfsame spot where he had
tossed away the Lamb & the legs of Ása-Thór shuddered
& he fell to his knees.

The feet of the tower of corpses trampled over the fallen
form of Ása-Thór & did retract & the tower of corpses
dropped onto Ása-Thór & crushed him & the tower of
corpses did sway mightily & did groan mightily.

& from over the horizon of the red & cloudy wastes of
Jupiter did the Lamb come a-tromping. The front leg of
the Lamb was broken & did show a sharp bone protruding
& the Lamb fell each time on this leg as it tromped & the
head of the Lamb hung by a string of flesh & the head did
flop as the Lamb tromped & blood poured from its neck
like unto a river & the hooves of the Lamb did slip as it
tromped. Yet the Lamb came a-tromping.

& the White Rider upon the White Horse & the army
of forty-eight thousand six-hundred twenty-one & the
tower of corpses all rejoiced at this sight & they did sing

the mighty hymn which was unlike any hymn & which was New to their Lord and all Lords.

The Lamb was among them & tried to stand on its broken leg which would not hold steady. All raised their palms high & continued to rejoice around the Lamb.

But the music of the hymn that was New was disturbed by a single voice. & all who were singing looked over their shoulders & did quiet their singing, but they could not find the voice that disturbed their hymn that was New.

Then the red & cloudy wastes of Jupiter began to churn. The hymn of all did fall to silence. The voice that was disturbing was muffled but began to grow clear & the voice came from the base of the tower of corpses & all who are well informed know that the voice was not of madness alone, or of fey alone, or of vengeance alone, or of blood-thirst alone. The voice was that which can no longer be understood because it came from an age that is no more.

It was the voice of a warrior & it did say this:

"For wrath. For glory."

The tower of corpses did shake. The tower of corpses did lift. The tower of corpses balanced on the back of Ása-Thór who grit his teeth & strained his legs & gnarled his face & gripped in both of his iron gauntlets the horrid hammer Mjölnir.

& Ása-Thór was screaming.

Ása-Thór swung Mjölnir above him & struck the tower of corpses that weighed on his back & a great crack split up the tower of corpses like unto lightning. Ása-Thór steadied Mjölnir again & struck again & the tower of corpses did explode & there was a rain of meat & the rain did not end.

& Ása-Thór was screaming.

Ása-Thór raised Mjölnir aloft & charged the White Rider upon the White Horse & the ranks of the army of forty-eight thousand six-hundred twenty-one. But the ranks did scatter & flee & wail in terror at the sight of Ása-Thór.

& Ása-Thór was screaming.

The White Rider upon the White Horse nocked a thin White arrow with his graceful hand & released it toward

Ása-Thór but Ása-Thór caught the arrow in the air with his iron gauntlet & crushed the arrow like unto a sliver of ice. Then Ása-Thór bore down upon the White Rider upon the White Horse & swung Mjölnir which did cave in the skull of the White Horse through its neck down to its shoulder & the White Horse did fall dead. The White Rider did scurry away, but Ása-Thór caught him up by his tall White Crown & tossed him to the ground. Then Ása-Thór stomped his boot on the chest of the White Rider & did watch his ribs split & his lungs flatten & his heart pop. & because of his anger he broke an arm off of the corpse of the White Rider with his teeth & ground the bones with his teeth.

& Ása-Thór was screaming.

& Ása-Thór stomped hard with his boot again & again & again & again & again & again & again & again & again & again until the corpse of the White Rider mixed with the rain of meat that did not end.

Then Ása-Thór did stop screaming & did glare at the Lamb & did breathe loudly with his nostrils for now there would be trouble for the Lamb.

The head of the Lamb which hung by a string of flesh did stare at Ása-Thór with four blank eyes & three eyes that were put out.

Ása-Thór did see that the Lamb wavered where it stood & he strode to the Lamb slowly & lifted the horrid hammer Mjölnir above his head & Ása-Thór asked the Lamb a question:

"Do you wish to speak a final curse? For I promise I will promptly kill you."

& the jaws of the Lamb did open & as the Lamb spoke & the Words of the Lamb were Holy that they did forge a gleaming sword from its tongue. & the tongue of the Lamb was Holy & the gleaming sword was Holy.

& Ása-Thór grabbed the blade of the gleaming sword with his iron gauntlet & ripped it out of the mouth of the Lamb & dashed it underfoot.

Then he brought down Mjölnir with the mightiest swing

onto the spine of the Lamb & knocked the Lamb through the surface of the red & cloudy wastes of Jupiter & through the hot core of the planet to the other side & the Lamb left only an abysmal hole in its wake.

Ása-Thór leapt into the abysmal hole to chase the corpse of the Lamb to collect a trophy from the remains of the Lamb & Ása-Thór did fall through the hot core of the planet & did fall out of the abysmal hole on the other side of the red & cloudy wastes of Jupiter & there did find the Lamb in shambles with shreds of flesh clinging to its bones which were exposed & its blood was spreading like unto a lake.

Yet the Lamb did stumble to its feet, again.

& at this sight Ása-Thór was filled with a great fury & he was dizzy & he did scream words which were this:

"Then I will eat you!"

& Ása-Thór waded through the lake of the blood of the Lamb & did gather the pieces of the Lamb into the palms of his iron gauntlets & did shove the Lamb into his mighty mouth.

& Ása-Thór chomped his mighty teeth.

Inside the world of the mouth of Ása-Thór, the tongue did push the flesh around like unto an dusky tide & the ivory mountains which hung in the heavens crashed down & rose again & crashed down again & crushed all the bones of the Lamb & broke all the horns of the Lamb & smashed all the eyes of the Lamb & ground all the organs of the Lamb. The vast pit of the throat swallowed the flesh of the Lamb & drank the blood of the Lamb.

& all fell into the mighty stomach of Ása-Thór.

Inside the world of the stomach of Ása-Thór, all was without form & was void. Darkness was upon the face of the deep. & from the body of the Lamb, a light grew & did grow. & the light changed all things & all things were forever changed.

Josh Woods is an author, editor, professor, and podcaster. He loves monsters, myth, storytelling, comedy, combat, and crafts. In addition to his novel, *The Black Palace*, he has edited three anthologies of fiction and has published genre and literary short stories, creative non-fiction, and craft essays in numerous journals, magazines, and collections. His awards include Outstanding Full-Time Faculty Member of the Year, Press 53 Open Awards for Genre Fiction, and multiple nominations for the Pushcart Prize. He teaches in Illinois and hails from Kentucky.

CPSIA information can be obtained
at www.ICGtesting.com
Printed in the USA
LVHW052302200319
611372LV00001B/126/P